# THE GHOST OF BLACKFEET NATION

### THE MYSTERY HOUSE SERIES, BOOK SIX

Eva Pohler

# Contents

*For the people of Blackfeet Nation who continue to fight to protect their sacred lands.*

# CHAPTER ONE

# A Midnight Emergency

D id I wake you?" Tanya asked Ellen over the phone.

Ellen sat up in her recliner—what used to be *Paul's* recliner—and paused the Netflix show she was watching. "I'm a night owl, remember? Everything okay?"

Tanya sounded frantic. "No. Dave's out of town. I called Sue, and she's on the way over, but now I'm worried she'll use her gun."

Ellen jumped to her feet. "Tanya? What's going on? Why would Sue use a gun?"

"Can I explain when you get here?" Tanya said. "I need you on my side."

"Do I need a bra for this?" Ellen was serious. Putting one on would slow her down.

"No. Just hurry."

Ellen ended the call, turned off the television, and slipped on her shoes, all the while wondering what could possibly be wrong at Tanya's house.

When Ellen arrived, she pulled up near the curb behind Sue's Porsche Taycan and scrambled to the front door.

Tanya opened it immediately. Her blonde hair was pulled back into a ponytail, and her blue eyes were red, as though she'd been crying. "It's out back."

"What is?" Ellen asked as she followed Tanya through the house. "Do I need a weapon?"

"God, no. It's just an armadillo."

Ellen grabbed Tanya's hand and turned her around to face her. "Wait a minute. Did you get me all worked up over an armadillo?"

Tears filled Tanya's eyes. "I think it's dying, and it's all my fault."

Ellen followed Tanya through the back door to the yard outside, where Sue was standing over a small cage containing an armadillo lying on its side.

"Is it still breathing?" Tanya asked Sue.

"Barely," she said as she pushed her brown bangs from her eyes. "You sure you don't want me to put it out of its misery?"

"Can someone explain to me what's going on?" Ellen insisted.

Through her tears, Tanya said, "Dave set out this trap, because something's been digging up my garden. Then he went out of town on Friday, and I forgot all about it, until this evening. This poor animal has been trapped inside that cage without food or water in this summer heat for maybe three days, and we need to save it. I tried putting water in there, but he didn't move."

"What's the plan?" Ellen asked.

"There's a place I know where we could release it. I was hoping one of you would drive, since I don't like driving at night."

Sue put her hands on her wide hips. "I could have helped you with that. You didn't need to drag Ellen here, too."

Tanya glanced nervously at Ellen.

"I don't mind," Ellen said. "I'll grab the cage. Sue better drive."

"Oh, that's right," Sue said. "I forgot about your new Jag."

Ellen had recently splurged on a shiny blue Jaguar, to mark the beginning of a new chapter in her life. It had been meant as a pick-me-up, but she should have known that material things, no matter how sexy and exciting, can only do so much.

"My trunk would be too hot," Ellen said. "Unless you don't mind sitting with the cage in the backseat."

Sue laughed. "I think I'd rather have raw eggs thrown at me."

Ellen and Tanya laughed as Ellen said, "We could arrange for that, I suppose."

"Maybe another time," Sue said. "Come on. I'll drive."

After they were on the road, Ellen asked from the back, "So, where is this place, Tanya?"

"Not too far," Tanya said from the passenger's seat. "It's that new area under development just north of us."

Sue blanched. "Won't there be tractors and other equipment tearing up the land? I wouldn't think that would be safe for the critter, but I'm no expert."

"Are you talking about where they're building that new strip mall right off of 281?" Ellen asked.

Tanya glanced back. "Yeah. Why?"

"Isn't it too close to the highway?" Ellen pointed out.

"I'm beginning to doubt that you care about that poor creature," Sue teased.

Tanya was soon in tears again. "What do we do, guys?"

"I vote for McAllister Park," Ellen said.

"That's a good idea." Tanya wiped her eyes with her sleeve. "Sorry, I'm just not thinking straight."

Sue did a U-turn and headed for the park. Fifteen minutes later, they stood beneath a tree canopy staring at the cage on the ground. The SUV was parked on the side of the road about fifty yards away. The park was quiet and empty. Ellen hoped the animal was still alive.

"I wish I had gloves," Tanya said as she reached out with a shaky hand. "I'm scared to touch it."

Sue rolled her eyes. "I'll do it."

She lifted the door to the cage and then uttered a hysterical cry as the armadillo jumped to its feet and scrambled past her and into the woods. Sue lost her balance and fell back onto the dirt.

Tanya leaned over her. "Are you okay?"

Sue busted out laughing. "That scared the heck out of me!"

Once she'd recovered from the shock, Ellen laughed, too, and offered Sue a hand. "Do armadillos play dead?"

"I guess so," Tanya said. "What a relief! I can't thank you guys enough! I'm sorry to have dragged you out here in the middle of the night. I owe you, big time."

"I know how you can thank me." Sue wiped the dirt and dried leaves from the back of her capri pants. "Why don't we grab a lemon loaf and a latte at Starbucks while you hear me out?"

Ellen followed her friends to the Taycan. "I hope you mean to drive through, because I'm not wearing a bra."

"Just carry your purse in front of you," Sue said.

Sue had to drive a bit further to find a Starbucks with a café that was open twenty-four hours, but she managed, and once they were sitting around a table with their lattes and cakes, she said, "Promise me that you'll keep an open mind."

Ellen and Tanya glanced at one another.

"I know you two wanted to pass on the project at Blackfeet Nation," Sue began, "but hear me out."

Ellen sighed. They'd already been over this a million times.

"Montana's too far," Tanya said.

"I get that you guys aren't interested in a vacation home near Glacier National Park—though it's still beyond me why. It's the crown of the continent, and the most beautiful place in America."

"I don't want to fly any more often than is necessary," Tanya reminded her. "Not after that crash landing in Brian's plane. We could have *died*."

Sue took a sip of her latte. "I'm not going to say all the things I've already said to try to change your mind—like the fact that the Blackfeet are practically giving the house away, along with the one hundred acres it sits on, or the fact that it's located right where the majestic Rocky Mountains meet the sweeping grassy plains, or the fact that the train is roomy and will boast amazing views along the way."

Tanya groaned as she took a bite of her lemon loaf.

For someone who wasn't going to say all the things she'd already said, Sue was saying quite a lot, Ellen thought as she sipped her latte.

"However," Sue paused dramatically. "I want the house for myself, and I'm asking you, begging you, as my dearest friends, to help me with the paranormal investigation. I'll take care of all the renovations. I'll pay for all of our expenses while we're there. And I'll make the three-day train ride worth your while."

Ellen lifted her brows. "How do you intend to do that?"

"I don't know yet, but I'll think of something."

Ellen and Tanya glanced dubiously at one another again, but Ellen was feeling less reluctant than she'd felt in the past. An entire year had passed since the Boulder City Hospital Hotel and Museum had been completed, and she was itching for another adventure.

A lot had happened since then. Ellen and Brian had broken up, Sue's mother Jan had passed away, and Tanya had fostered a five and six-year-old brother and sister, who'd just been returned to their mother upon her release from prison. All three of their hearts had been broken.

"I wasn't going to play the grief card," Sue said with tears in her eyes, "but I need to get away."

Ellen bit her bottom lip, recalling how she had felt in the wake of Paul's death. She understood all too well.

"I need to get away from San Antonio," Sue said, breaking down. "I need a distraction."

Tanya reached across the table to squeeze Sue's hand. "I still miss my mother, but it does get easier."

Ellen felt a tinge of guilt for not thinking of her own mother. She'd thought only of Paul.

"At least we finally found someone to take over at the Gold House," Sue said. "That was a nightmare, wasn't it?"

"I'll go with you," Ellen blurted out. "I'll help you with the investigation, and, if you want, the renovation, too."

Sue's brows shot up. "Really? Does that mean you want to go in with me?"

"I don't know yet," Ellen said. "I'll need to see the house and the property first."

"Of course."

They turned to Tanya, who said, "Thanks a lot for throwing me under the bus, Ellen."

"Not under the bus," she said. "On the *train*. Come on. I'm anxious to see how Sue plans to make it worth our while."

Sue lifted her brows. "I guess you're going to hold me to it, even in my grief."

Tanya shook her head. "She's just teasing. Your company is enough to make it worth our while. Wouldn't you agree, Ellen?"

Ellen cocked her head to the side. "Let me get back to you on that."

Sue lobbed a piece of her lemon loaf at Ellen's face. The cake bounced off Ellen's nose and onto the floor.

"Darn," Sue said. "I wanted that bite. Thanks for getting me all riled up."

The three friends laughed.

A week later, in mid-July, as Ellen boarded the train with her friends, she felt a sense of panic. She had forgotten to call her kids to let them know that she was leaving town. When Paul was still alive, she hadn't felt it was necessary to tell her kids about her every move. It had been the same while she was dating Brian. But now there was no one waiting for her at home. If something were to happen to her and to her friends—if the train crashed and killed them—there would be no one alive who'd be aware of her absence for however long it would take the police to notify the family.

As she made her way to her seat, she chastised herself for being silly. Nothing was going to happen to them; yet it felt strange that there was no one waiting for her to check in, to touch base, to hear about her day.

Once she was settled next to Tanya in her seat with Sue sitting across the aisle from her, Ellen took out her phone and texted her kids. The panic in her chest lessened.

Then Sue asked, "Do they serve margaritas on this train?"

Ellen smiled. "I believe they do."

Sue's big brown eyes brightened.

"This is better than the sleeper room, don't you think?" Tanya asked. "These seats go all the way back, and no one has to sleep on top."

"From what I've heard, Ellen likes being on top," Sue teased.

"I plan to spend most of the trip in the sightseer lounge anyway," Ellen said, ignoring her friend's crass remark.

"Did you remember to download the national park podcast I told you about?" Sue asked.

"I'll do that now," Ellen said.

Ellen thought of Brian. They'd parted ways six months ago at a national park. She hoped that fact wouldn't ruin all national parks for her.

No. She wouldn't let it, she thought, as tears sprang to her eyes.

Once the train was underway, Tanya leaned forward and asked Sue, "So, what do you know about this property, anyway?"

"It's called Talks to Buffalo Lodge. It's a two-story ranch that was built in 1890 and has been haunted since the 1940s, if not earlier," Sue said. "And it's been vacant since the seventies."

"Since the seventies? No wonder the Blackfeet Nation is anxious to find an owner," Ellen said.

"Do you know anything about the haunting?" Tanya asked. "Is it one ghost or multiple? What have you heard?"

"It's not good," Sue said. "I wish I could say that no one died there."

Ellen glanced at Tanya, whose brows had lifted and whose jaw had dropped open.

"Why are you just now telling me this?" Tanya wanted to know.

"You know the answer to that question," Sue said, avoiding their gaze.

Tanya's face turned red, and she closed her mouth, her lips forming a straight line.

"Give her a chance to explain," Ellen said to Tanya, but Tanya said nothing in reply.

Sue leaned across the aisle with a hand on Ellen's armrest. "Well, according to the tribal secretary, the house was occupied by six different owners—all Blackfeet except for the most recent owner. The house was built in 1890 by its first owner and namesake, Talks to Buffalo. He and his wife lived there until they died—he around 1930 and she sometime in the early forties. The house was sold to another Blackfeet family with two children—a son and a daughter. They later claimed their son was possessed by an evil spirit for three or four years before it eventually took him one night in his sleep."

Tanya's face paled. "Unbelievable."

Ellen turned to Sue. "You should have told her."

"I tried to talk to both of you about the house," Sue said, "but you shut me down every time."

"That was before we agreed to come along," Ellen said. "You should have told us after we agreed but before we committed—before we got on this train."

"Are you saying you want to turn around and go home?" Sue asked.

Ellen glanced at Tanya, whose back was to her as she stared out the window at the passing buildings in downtown San Antonio.

Ellen said, "They won't stop the train. We'd have to wait to get off in Dallas."

Tanya turned to look at her. "Is that what you want?"

Ellen bit her bottom lip and shook her head. "We've been through this kind of thing before, and we're stronger for it. *You're* stronger for it."

Tanya wiped her eyes. "*Am* I?"

"Yes," Ellen said. "But we'll understand if you want to get off and turn around."

"I would have liked the choice before *now.*"

"I know. I'm sorry."

Sue leaned across the aisle again. "*I'm* the one who's sorry, Tanya. Truly. I should have told you. I just really wanted you to come, be-cause…" Sue broke down into tears. "Well, because it wouldn't be the same without you."

Tanya said nothing for several seconds before Ellen asked her, "What are you going to do?"

"I don't know yet. I guess I have a lot of time to think about it. Sue may as well tell us the rest of what she knows."

Sue dried her eyes and collected herself before continuing her story. "Okay. Let's see. After Talks to Buffalo and his wife, and then the fami-ly with the son who died, there was a family who lived there in the early fifties. Something similar happened to their son, only he didn't die. They moved away, off the reservation, to live with friends in another state, where they got medical treatment for the boy."

"That's a relief," Ellen said.

"A couple without any children occupied the house from 1954 through 1960. They reported years of harassment—furniture being rear-ranged, cabinets and drawers being opened, clothes pulled from their hangers, and stuff like that."

"No possession?" Ellen asked.

Sue shook her head. "But after six years, they were tired of it and moved. The fifth family had two sons, and both boys suffered and near-ly died before the family moved in the late sixties."

Tanya shuddered. "Geez."

"The most recent owner was a single man in his forties, I think," Sue said. "He lived there until he died of a heart attack in 1973. He had no living relatives or close friends, so no one knows if he ever experienced anything unusual, or if his death was anything more than a regular heart attack."

"Hopefully, that's all it was," Ellen said.

"No one's occupied the house since 1973," Sue said. "The tribe has tried to sell it many times, but its reputation keeps potential buyers away. We're the first people to ask to look at the property in over ten years."

"Wow." Ellen could only imagine the condition the house must be in, to have been vacant for so long. "Does it have running water and electricity?"

"The tribal secretary wasn't sure when I asked," Sue replied. "But either way, this property is a steal. And from what I can tell using Google Earth, it has amazing views, not to mention its proximity to the park."

Ellen was glad they had decided to ship their equipment to Glacier Park Lodge rather than lug it around on the train. Spirits capable of possession and possibly murder would require every instrument and machine they had for a proper investigation. She'd been an emotional wreck for months and wasn't sure she was up for the challenge, but she refused to turn back, and she hoped Tanya would feel the same.

"I'll go with you to the park," Tanya finally said. "I'm dying to see it. But I don't know if I want to help with the paranormal investigation. I'll think about it."

"Thank you," Sue said. "Just having you along on the trip makes all the difference."

Ellen noticed the corners of Tanya's mouth lift into a barely perceptible smile.

"Sue's right," Ellen said. "You do what you feel comfortable doing. You don't need to step foot on the reservation."

"I do if we still plan to hit the casino," she said, her face back to its normal color.

"True," Ellen said with a laugh. "And we still plan to do that. Don't we, Sue?"

"Absolutely." Sue grinned. "Now, let's see about those margaritas!"

# CHAPTER TWO

# Glacier National Park

Glacier Park Lodge was within walking distance of the station. As Ellen led the way across the parking lot in the late afternoon, pulling her luggage behind her, she breathed in the cool mountain air—a pleasant change from the hot, humid days in San Antonio. Even in July, the air was crisp and dry and delightful here, and the mountain views exhilarated and rejuvenated her.

"Look!" Tanya cried. "Bighorn sheep!"

Ellen followed Tanya's finger across the parking lot, to where two Bighorn sheep were meandering between parked cars, as if the parking lot were a natural part of the landscape.

"Oh, wow!" Sue said. "They must be used to all of this."

As they stopped to watch the animals, Ellen wanted nothing more than to pull out her sketch pad and capture the moment. Instead, she plucked her phone from her purse and snapped a photo.

"We'll have plenty of time for that," Sue said of the photo. "Let's get checked in, shall we?"

Ellen was pleased by the high ceilings built from massive firs—at least forty-feet high—in the lobby of Glacier Park Lodge and by the huge stone fireplace in the middle of the room, surrounded by couches and chairs and brightly colored pillows. Later, she was even more pleased by the views from her balcony looking out onto the Rocky Mountains. The floor-to-ceiling windows and sliding balcony door made it possible for her to enjoy the views from indoors, too.

Her paranormal investigative equipment had been brought up and set down in the middle of the room. She now shoved the boxes containing her full-spectrum cameras, passive infrared motion detectors, large EMF recorder, and the electromagnetic pump under the table and desk and put her duffle bag of thermometers, batteries, handheld EMF detectors, sketch pad, and Ouija Board onto the floor of the closet. Not for the first time, she thought about how far she'd come since their very first flip—the Gold House in San Antonio. She'd been so adamant that there were no such things as ghosts, and although they had discovered that more than a ghost was contributing to the strange phenomena there, her world had been turned upside down. Now, here she was, nearly five years later, one of the country's leading experts in paranormal studies. After their project in Boulder City, she and her friends had been interviewed on two of the three major television networks and had articles written about them in multiple major publications.

As the hours passed, the temperature dropped from the mid-seventies to the low sixties. Ellen wondered why she spent most summers in the Texas heat when she could go anywhere in the world. Her kids were living their own lives and rarely visited anymore. What was keeping her at home?

She and Brian had planned to travel the world together. That had ended six months ago not far from where she was now standing, one state away at Yellowstone National Park.

On Wednesday morning, Ellen and her friends met their tour guide—a man named Rich Falcon—before dawn in the lodge parking lot, where they climbed into his van and headed west to Lake McDonald.

From behind the wheel, their driver, who looked to be in his mid to late sixties and who wore his long white hair pulled back in a ponytail at the nape of his neck, asked, "Is this your first visit to Glacier National Park?" His voice was gravelly, and he had a habit of nodding his head as he spoke.

"It is," Sue said in the middle seat beside Tanya. "Are you from this area?"

"Yes," the man replied as he turned onto the main road. "My ancestors lived here more than ten thousand years ago. I was born and raised here and will eventually die here."

"Sounds like I picked the right guide then," Sue said with a smile.

"I'm not like any other guide," he said with a sideways glance and another nod of his head. "It took me a long time to get my license approved by the corporation that controls most of the businesses around here. They didn't want me to tell the stories of my people."

"I wonder why," Tanya said.

"Greed and intolerance," he replied. "They tried to make us invisible and to disconnect us from what was our land for thousands of years."

"I'm glad to hear that things are changing," Ellen said from the third seat.

"That's the one constant in this world," he said as he made another turn. "Change. And it's not always for the better."

"He's quite a philosopher," Sue whispered.

Tanya leaned forward. "Why do they call the road you're taking us to *Going to the Sun Road*?"

"It's named for Going to the Sun *Mountain*," he said. He spoke with a rhythmic cadence that seemed in tune with his nods. "You see, my people believe that the Sun is the Creator. We call him Napi, or Old Man. Further north of here is another mountain called Chief Mountain. We Blackfeet believe it was the only land not submerged in water at the beginning of time. And we believe that the end of time will come with its destruction. To us, it's the center of the earth."

"How interesting," Sue said.

"We call this whole area here the backbone of the earth," he added. Then he pointed northwest and said, "That's Going to the Sun Mountain. Going to the Sun Road will lead us to it. A long time ago, one of my people, named Tail Feathers, said that that mountain would be the best place for a spirit quest, for going to the Sun. And that's how it got its name."

"Do your people still go on spirit quests?" Tanya asked.

"Oh, yes. It's an important part of our way of life. We go to a sacred place south of here, to an area known as Badger-Two Medicine, where Napi created the land and all the people who inhabit it."

"Is it part of the reservation?" Tanya asked.

"Unfortunately, no," he said. "In 1895, we were promised that the Badger-Two Medicine would be a communal space that everyone could use for hunting, fishing, and other recreational activities. It's where we practiced many of our religious rituals and ceremonies when such things were outlawed. We continue to do so today."

"Wait," Ellen interrupted. "Are you saying it was against the law at one time to practice your religion?"

"That's exactly what I'm saying," Rich Falcon said with an emphatic nod. "There was a time when being an Indian was considered bad. From about 1890 to the late seventies, we could only be ourselves in secret."

"That's horrible," Tanya said.

"How ironic, considering that the earliest immigrants came here to escape religious persecution," Sue pointed out.

"It gets worse," Rich said as he turned along the curving road. "In the early 1980s, during the Reagan administration, leases were granted to oil and gas companies that would allow drilling in the Badger-Two Medicine."

"But what about the agreement?" Tanya asked.

"It was ignored. We fought against the oil companies for decades and put a halt to their plans. Just this year, we finally got the US government to pull the last of the fifteen original leases. It only took us forty years."

Ellen wondered how she'd never heard about the battle between the oil companies and the native people.

"Your tribe must be relieved to have that behind you," Sue said.

"We won't be at peace until we get our bill passed—a bill to protect the land as a cultural heritage area, so it won't ever be vulnerable to drilling or other kinds of development again. In fact, there's one oil and gas company, Solonex, run by a man named Sidney Longfellow, that won't let it go. They're suing the federal government for breach of contract, hoping to get their lease reinstated."

"Oh, no," Tanya said. "Do you think they have a chance of winning?"

"There's no telling," their driver said.

Ellen gazed across the landscape to the south, where the plains became rolling hills. "That's the Badger-Two Medicine, out there?"

"Beyond those hills," he said.

"Can people who aren't members of the tribe go on spirit quests?" Ellen asked, wondering if the experience might help her to fill the gaping hole in her heart.

"Sometimes, with permission and guidance," he said. "It's usually for men, but in recent years, women have gone on spirit quests, too."

"I'm glad to hear that the tribe is keeping up with the times," Sue said.

They rode in silence for many minutes. The sun was just beginning to rise when they finally turned onto Going to the Sun Road and drove through the west entrance of the park toward Apgar Village, where they stopped to use the restroom and to buy a few postcards and cups of coffee.

"Oh, look," Sue said, holding up a spray bottle that read *Bear Assault Deterrent Spray.* "We should each buy one of these, just in case."

Ellen shook her head. "It's a scam and a waste of money. Don't fall for it, Sue."

"You'll feel differently if we come upon a Grizzly," Sue said.

Rich, who had overheard the conversation from a few feet away, said, "The best thing to do when faced with a bear is to talk softly to it as you slowly back away. Don't run, don't scream, and don't attack, even with that spray bottle."

"I'd listen to *him*," Tanya said.

Sue returned the spray back to the rack. "I guess he's the expert. Plus, if worse comes to worse, I can always use my gun."

They followed Rich from the center to a pier overlooking the lake, where five mountain peaks nestled together beyond the shoreline.

By seven a.m., they were back on the road and driving toward Lake McDonald Lodge. Since the plan was to drive along Going to the Sun Road as the sun rose in the east, they didn't stop until they'd passed the lodge and reached the roaring McDonald Falls. They snapped a few photos before continuing onward.

The sunrise over the mountains was breathtaking. Rich Falcon pulled over a few times along the way to show them such sights as a valley full of antelope, a stream where two large moose had a morning drink, and cascades of turquoise rapids tumbling across the river rocks.

In some places, the road seemed dangerously narrow with the flat rock face of a mountain on one side and a dangerously steep drop of hundreds of feet on the other. Ellen noticed Tanya clutching her safety harness and Sue leaning away from her window and the deep ravine. Only their driver seemed unaffected by the perilous path.

On the way to another stop at the Big Bend pullout, they drove past a stretch of rock, at least a hundred feet long, with cascading water dripping from the flat face of a mountain.

"This is known as Weeping Wall," Rich Falcon said.

Not far from Weeping Wall, he parked and led them down a paved path past purple wildflowers to a breathtaking view of four mountains nested together behind a deep valley where white flowers bloomed.

As beautiful as the landscape was, Ellen was drawn back to the flat-faced mountain on the opposite side of the road with its never-ending tears. While her friends remained behind at the Big Bend overlook, Ellen trekked past parked cars to get closer to Weeping Wall.

Ellen stood there, mesmerized, as tears of her own seeped from the corners of her eyes and slipped down her cheeks, just as the natural springs leaked from the stone wall and onto passing cars. The weeping wall symbolized what she was feeling. Her world was changing in ways she couldn't control. Her parents were dead. Her husband was dead. Her children were living lives of their own, away from her. She and her brother rarely saw one another. She was untethered. If it weren't for Sue and Tanya, she'd feel utterly alone in the world. It took an act of bravery to face life in such a state—bravery and a lot of tears.

It was after nine o'clock in the morning when they reached the highest point of Going to the Sun Road at Logan Pass on the continental divide. They stopped to walk along a few of the trails to soak in the majesty before heading another five miles north to eat breakfast in the Ptarmigan Dining Room at Many Glacier Hotel, overlooking Swiftcurrent Lake and the snow-covered mountains beyond it.

They invited Rich Falcon to join them, but he said he wasn't hungry and would be waiting outside on the deck, having a smoke.

"I think I understand the meaning of the word *medicine*, as the Blackfeet and other tribes use it," Ellen said over her pancakes. "This place feels like much needed medicine for my soul."

"I know what you mean," Tanya agreed.

Sue took a sip of her coffee before saying, "You still haven't really explained why you and Brian aren't seeing each other anymore. Are you officially broken up? Or has he just been super busy?"

Ellen's stomach clenched.

"Sue," Tanya chastised.

"Excuse me for being worried about our dearest friend," Sue said, as if concern and not curiosity, were the reason for her questions.

Ellen took a deep breath. She'd planned to talk to them about it at some point on the trip, but she'd hoped to be the one to broach the subject. As she pushed a bite of pancake around on her plate, she fought tears. Her friends were quiet. Whether they were silenced by feelings of awkwardness or were patiently waiting for Ellen to reply, she didn't know.

Finally, Ellen said, "Brian accused me of keeping him at arm's length." She put down her fork and wiped her mouth with her napkin. "And he was right."

Her friends looked at her with sympathetic frowns, but she avoided their gaze as she got up and excused herself before finding the restroom. She entered a stall, sat on the commode, and closed her eyes, where she saw Weeping Wall, as if she were standing in front of it.

Ellen and her friends spent the rest of the day meandering along the trails at Saint Mary Lake, where they visited more amazing falls and took in more spectacular mountain vistas. Although the area was full of tourists, there were plenty of secluded places along the paths where Ellen and her friends felt fully immersed in nature.

Ellen kept expecting Sue to complain about her hurting feet, or her shortness of breath, or her increased appetite from the exercise; instead, she was the perfect picture of congeniality. Ellen supposed her friend was trying to make up for what had happened at breakfast. As the hours passed, Ellen was less and less aware of the hole in her heart and more and more awed by the beauty surrounding her. By the time Rich Falcon met up with them at the Saint Mary Visitor Center to return them to Glacier Park Lodge, she felt giddy with happiness.

"Before we leave this place, I want to show you something," Rich said as he led them from the parking lot in the opposite direction of the lake and visitor center, toward a wooded area.

"What is it?" Sue asked.

"Trust me. You want to see this."

"Can you make it, Sue?" Tanya asked. "How are your feet?"

"I guess we're about to find out," she said, "though this does seem off the beaten path."

"It is," Rich said. "Like I told you, I'm not like the other guides. Just stay close."

Ellen exchanged worried glances with her friends.

Not wanting to offend their guide, Ellen said nothing as she followed him away from civilization and into the thick forest, thinking the whole while that this was exactly how serial killers lured their victims into out-of-the-way places.

After about ten minutes of traipsing beneath the tall firs and hemlocks, Rich said in a low voice, "Just beyond this stretch of trees is a place where grizzlies come to fish."

Ellen stopped in her tracks and whispered, "Did you say grizzlies? As in Grizzly *bears?*"

Rich Falcon lifted his brows and smiled. "What other kind of grizzlies are there?"

Sue and Tanya stopped too.

Tanya said, "I think we should head back."

"Will you trust me?" he asked them.

"No offense, Rich, but we don't know you," Sue said.

"If you can see them while they're in the lake, they won't bother you," he said. "And this time of day, I guarantee you they're in the lake."

Ellen felt a chill of excitement—or perhaps of hysteria—crawl down her back. "You guarantee it?"

"I do," he said with a smile.

"I'm going back," Tanya said, as she turned toward the Visitor Center.

Ellen suddenly wanted to see the grizzlies. She wanted it more than she'd wanted anything in the past several months. She turned to Sue. "I'm going with Rich. Are you?"

"I don't think this is a good idea," Sue said.

"Then wait here," Ellen said before nodding to Rich to lead the way.

"Well, hell," Sue said. "I feel responsible for you. If you're going, I guess I'm going, too."

Ellen giggled. "You only live once."

"And that's supposed to be an argument *in favor* of going?" Sue asked.

Ellen giggled again. The hole in her heart seemed nothing but a tiny pinpoint as the fear, excitement, and thrill of adventure took possession of her.

Rich slowed his pace and lightened his footfalls before whispering, "From here on out, don't speak."

The brush became thick before the lake came into view. At first, Ellen saw nothing but more mountain vistas and sparkling water. It wasn't until Sue covered her mouth and gasped that Ellen saw four grizzlies to the east fishing in the shallow part of the lake not far from its banks—a mother and three cubs.

Their light-brown fur appeared golden blond in the bright sunshine. One of the cubs seemed to be playing more than fishing as it tumbled forward, like an acrobat performing a somersault, before popping up from the water to hover close to its mother and siblings.

The mother scoured the lake for trout. When she finally caught one in her fierce teeth, Ellen expected her to feed her cubs, but she ate it without sharing so much as a bite.

Ellen held her breath when the bears moved along the shore in their direction. Then the mother climbed onto the bank and sat up on her hind legs to look and sniff around. Did she smell the onlookers? Sue took a few careful steps back.

Ellen was about to follow Sue's lead when the mother bear suddenly plopped onto her back to dry in the sun as the cubs found a teat and nursed. Ellen covered her mouth to stifle the joyful laughter bubbling in her throat. It was a sweet, adorable sight and an amazing privilege to behold it.

Once they were in the van and headed back to Glacier Park Lodge, Sue leaned forward and asked Rich Falcon, "Have you ever heard of Talks to Buffalo Lodge?"

"Of course," he said. "Everyone who lives on the reservation has heard of it. It's the most haunted place in Montana."

Sue glanced back at Ellen before turning back to Rich. "Well, I'm going to look at it tomorrow. I'm thinking of buying it."

"You're a brave woman," he said. "My people avoid that area like the plague."

Ellen said, "We're paranormal investigators. We have a lot of experience with haunted places."

"Good," he said. "You'll need it."

A moment later he asked, "So when will you be undergoing the purification ritual?"

"The what?" Ellen asked.

Sue gave her a sheepish grin. "I hadn't told my friends about that yet."

Tanya frowned. "About what?"

"The tribal secretary said that, before she can show us the property, we'll need to undergo a purification ceremony," Sue explained. "It's for our own protection, she said."

"What's a purification ceremony?" Ellen asked.

"I guess you're about to find out," Rich Falcon said with a hearty laugh.

# CHAPTER THREE

# Badger-Two Medicine

That night, Ellen had a hard time falling asleep, even though her room and the bed were quite comfortable, and the views, which she could see without crawling out from beneath the covers, were breathtaking. Even at night, the moon and starlight washed over the surrounding white mountain peaks with iridescent brilliance.

She hadn't slept well in months. As had become her habit every night, she ate ten milligrams of melatonin with a glass of red wine and turned on the television. She used her Amazon Prime account to re-watch episodes of *Downton Abbey* until she fell asleep.

It seemed as if only a few moments had passed when her morning alarm on her phone went off. She groaned.

After she'd managed to get out of bed and to wash her face at the bathroom sink, she was astonished to see Weeping Wall in her bathroom mirror. She blinked, and it vanished.

By the time she had joined her friends in the lodge restaurant for breakfast, she had come alive again. A cup of coffee was all it took. She and her friends went through the buffet line to fill their plates before returning to their table beside an enormous window with more incredible mountain views.

"Eat up," Sue said. "We'll be fasting all afternoon, as part of the purification ceremony."

"I thought we were supposed to fast all day," Tanya said. "Isn't that what Rich Falcon said yesterday?"

"I don't think so," Sue said as she took a bite of her Belgium waffle, which was sprinkled with powdered sugar. "Anyway, it's too late now."

The pancakes seemed to melt in Ellen's mouth. "If I'm not careful, I'm going to gain back that twenty pounds that always seem to come back."

"Twenty pounds is nothing," Sue said. "I gain that much just by drinking a glass of water."

Ellen doubted that was true, but she smiled and took a sip of her coffee.

After breakfast, Ellen and her friends rode the hotel shuttle to the reservation tribal headquarters. The reservation reminded Ellen of the old army and air force bases in San Antonio. The land was flat and had relatively few trees compared to the surrounding landscape. The houses sat close to the road and were mostly small bungalows with no fencing or landscaping. The shuttle drove past an abandoned basketball park surrounded by a chain-link fence before coming upon a long rectangular building without any signage. Ellen thought it could be a nursing home or a school. There was no way of knowing. Beyond it was another long rectangular building that resembled an old motel.

"Here we are," their driver said as he pulled into a parking space. "Just give me a call when you're ready to be picked up."

"This is the tribal headquarters?" Sue asked.

"Yes, ma'am," the driver said.

Ellen followed the others from the shuttle. They stood beneath the hot summer sun surrounded by dust.

"Which way do we go?" Ellen asked Sue.

Sue looked this way and that. "I have no idea which is the front door."

"Should we try that one?" Tanya pointed to the door in the center of the building.

Sue shrugged. "Seems as good a try as any."

They entered a corridor that reminded Ellen of a middle school. Even the sign that read, "Main Office," had the feel of a school.

Before they reached the main office, an old man emerged from the door with a smile on his face.

"You should have worn better shoes," he said to Sue.

He was about her height and wore his short white hair combed to one side. His dark eyes were like black pebbles on a mostly hairless face. His mouth barely moved when he spoke, and his teeth occasionally whistled. "Those sandals won't be comfortable."

"They're my most comfortable shoes," Sue said. "I have feet problems, and I had these made especially for me."

Two other men joined the first in the hallway beside Ellen and her friends.

"You'll want to wear socks with them, then," the first man continued. His thin lips formed a natural smile as he spoke, giving the impression that he was always smiling. "We'll be walking through all kinds of terrain today, and you won't want your skin exposed to the elements."

Ellen was glad that she had worn her Vans. Tanya had worn sneakers. The three men wore jeans and boots, along with their long-sleeved button-down shirts, which, to Ellen, seemed like the wrong attire for the summer heat.

"You aren't the tribal secretary," Sue said to the first man.

"No," he said. "My name is Eric Old Person. I'm the chief of Blackfeet Nation."

"Oh," Sue glanced nervously at Ellen and Tanya. "How nice to meet you. We weren't expecting to meet royalty today."

The three men laughed.

"The chief likes to be present at any ceremonies conducted with non-Indians," the tallest of the three men explained in his deep baritone voice. Then he offered his hand. "Hello. I'm Jack Stone. And I live just around the corner. I'll grab you a pair of socks on our way out."

Although he was mostly bald, he had a strong jawline and attractive eyes beneath dark, bushy brows.

"That's awfully nice," Sue said with a smitten look on her face. Then she whispered to Ellen, "He fills out his jeans nicely, doesn't he?"

"You're going to get into trouble one of these days," Ellen whispered back.

The third man was also tall but wiry and was wearing a cowboy hat over his long dark hair, which fell in a single braid down his back. He reached out his hand and said, "I'm Terry Murray."

"It's nice to meet you," Ellen said.

They followed the men to a minivan, where Terry Murray took the driver's seat as Jack Stone opened the sliding backdoor for the ladies.

Eric Old Person sat in the front passenger seat. Jack Stone helped Tanya and Sue into the middle seat before joining Ellen in the third. Sue glanced back at Ellen with raised brows. Ellen blushed, worried the look hadn't gone unnoticed by Jack. She wanted to smack her friend upside the head but forced a smile instead as Jack settled into the seat beside her.

"I'm looking forward to the tour of your reservation," Sue said to the chief. "Especially since I may be its newest resident."

"Let's not get ahead of ourselves," Eric Old Person said. "There's no need for a tour, unless you plan to purchase the property, and you can't set foot on the property until you've been purified."

Sue's smile faded as she glanced back at Ellen.

"It's for your protection," Jack Stone explained. "You wouldn't want to face the evil at Talks to Buffalo Lodge without first arming yourself with purity."

"I suppose not," Sue said.

"Can you tell us more about the evil spirit?" Tanya asked Jack as Terry pulled away from the headquarters and onto the road. "Have you experienced anything paranormal there, personally?"

From the front seat, Eric Old Person said, "You must understand that we believe all spirits, good and evil, dwell alongside us. They often reach out to us—sometimes through animals or plants or other objects. We don't consider them *paranormal.* We consider them *normal.* You understand?"

"I think I do," Tanya said. "Thanks for explaining that."

"Having said that," the chief added, "I must admit that I've never encountered anything more sinister or violent than the evil spirit that resides at Talks to Buffalo Lodge."

Tanya glanced back at Ellen with a pale face. Ellen and Sue also exchanged worried looks.

"Should we be afraid for our lives?" Sue asked the men.

"The purification ritual will help," the chief said.

Ellen didn't find the chief's answer reassuring—not one bit. She began to wonder what horrible danger Sue had gotten them into.

Terry Murray stopped at a corner bungalow, where Jack jumped out, saying, "Be right back."

The rest of them sat in awkward silence as the dust from road settled, until Jack returned with a pair of white tube socks, which he handed to Sue.

"Thank you," Sue said, sounding less than grateful, as though they weren't quite up to her standards.

"Don't worry, they're clean," Jack said with a laugh.

A few moments later, as they pulled from the reservation, Ellen turned to Jack. "So, tell me about your sweat lodge. Is it very big?"

Jack laughed. "It's not a permanent structure. Is that what you thought? You imagined a lodge with a big fireplace and tall ceilings, like the one you're staying at in East Glacier Park?"

Ellen shrugged. "Well, not exactly."

"There are no manmade structures, roads, or infrastructures of any kind in Badger-Two Medicine," Jack said. "When you walk along the river, or across the plains, or along the mountainside, or through the trees, you see exactly what people ten thousand years ago would have seen. Nothing's changed."

"Then what is the sweat lodge?" Sue asked. "A cave?"

The men upfront laughed.

"Not a cave," Jack said. "You have to build it. It's part of the ritual."

"Wait. What?" Sue asked.

"When you say, 'you have to build it,'" Ellen asked, "do you mean *us*? My friends and I?"

"We're here to help," Terry Murray said as he turned down another road leading to the highway.

"Well, that's a relief," Sue said sarcastically. "You do realize that my friends and I are approaching sixty?"

"I'm sixty-three," Jack said. "And Terry is nearly sixty, aren't you, bud?"

"I turn sixty in December," their driver said.

"And I'm seventy-eight," Eric Old Person said. "Surely if I can do it…"

"You don't look your age," Sue said.

"Thank you," the chief said. "It comes from routinely being in nature. Walking, climbing, breathing—it's all good for your soul as well as your body."

"I wouldn't know," Sue said in a feeble attempt to get a laugh.

"I suppose I can wait in the car," Tanya said with a smile, "since I'm not planning on setting foot on the property."

"Do you really want to miss all the fun?" Ellen asked, fighting a fit of giggles.

Tanya giggled, too. "I think I'll be okay."

"No, Tanya," Sue insisted. "You're in the best shape of the three of us. Plus, you like being in nature. You said you want to go on a vision quest, didn't you?"

"All vision quests begin with a purification ceremony," Jack said. "So, consider this practice."

Ellen burst into laughter. "I suppose we're in for it, now. Come on, Sue. Don't look so out of sorts. You might get to hold a power tool."

"No power tools," Terry Murray said as he merged onto the highway. "We take very little onto the land, and we take nothing from it, except what we hunt, to nourish our bodies."

"Aren't we bringing tools?" Ellen asked Jack beside her.

"Just an ax and a saw and some rope," Jack said.

"And our knives," Terry Murray added.

"You see," Eric Old Person began, "Sun and Moon told one of the very first of our people how to make the sweat lodge. The young man was known as Scarface. And when he returned from living in the sky with Morning Star, he became known as Mistaken-For-Morning-Star, because his scar was gone, and he was as beautiful as Morning Star. He taught the rest of us what Creator wants us to do. We've been doing it this way for thousands of years."

Sue gave Ellen a look of fright. "We may be in for a lot more than we bargained for."

"You think?" Ellen continued to fight the giggles.

Terry Murray parked the van on the side of a road near a long line of pine trees. After everyone but Sue climbed out, they gathered supplies from the back of the van while Sue pulled on the tube socks. Along with the saw and ax were three canteens, a ceremonial pipe, a black forked stick with a leather handle, dozens of short lengths of rope wound together in a bag made of netting, and several colorful woven blankets and animal skins.

"What are those for?" Ellen asked, pointing to the blankets and skins.

"Those will be the walls of our sweat lodge," Eric Old Person replied as he took out the pipe. "See this? It's very, very old and was given to us by the Creator. He uses it to speak with us."

"I can't wait to hear what he has to say," Ellen said.

"Now, don't laugh," Sue said, as she finally climbed from the van wearing her sandals over the socks. "I know I'm not the most fashionable-looking among us."

"You're much better off than you were," Jack said, as he handed her a blanket to carry.

Sue turned to Tanya, who already had a blanket thrown over her shoulder. "I'm glad you decided to come along."

"I'm sure you are," Tanya teased. "Or you'd be carrying this one, too."

As the chief led the way through the trees and thick underbrush, Terry Murray, who carried the forked stick and bag of netting over one shoulder, said, "Everything has to be gathered a certain way. You want round stones for the coals. Keep an eye out for them. You can collect them in your blankets."

"And you want thin but strong willow branches for the frame," Jack added. "It would be best if *you* picked out the poles, since this is for your purification, but I'll guide you."

"We also need sage for the floor," Eric Old Person said. "Sage grows all over the area, so let us know when you spot some. You know what sage is, don't you?"

Sue chuckled. "We use it all the time, though it's usually dried and tied into a smudge stick."

"I know what it looks like," Tanya said.

"Then it's good thing you came," Sue added.

The chief added, "The Creator will lead you to the right rocks, to the right branches, and to the right sage. Then, if he so wishes, he will use those elements to make his message clear to you."

"Watch your step," Jack said. "We avoid making trails by entering from a different way as often as we can. Watch out for this thorny bush."

Jack held a branch to the side while the ladies passed through.

"Thanks," Ellen said. Then to Sue, she said, "I bet you're glad for those socks now."

"Don't rub it in," Sue complained.

Once they emerged from the pines, they stood on the top of a hillside overlooking a beautiful valley, with the Missouri River running through it.

"Wow," Ellen said.

"Jews, Christians, and Muslims go to a building to worship," Terry Murray said. "But we go here. Badger-Two Medicine is our place of worship."

"And it's not just for Sundays," Jack added.

On the other side of the river, the mountains stood in the distance, their white peaks reaching toward a deep blue sky.

"Since there aren't many trees below, should we gather our branches before we go down?" Ellen asked.

"There are a few trees closer to the river," Jack said. "It might be easier on you not to have to carry them so far."

"That sounds good to me," Sue said.

"But if you feel called to a particular branch," the chief said, "then, by all means, speak up."

The grassy slope down toward the river was steep. Ellen kept an eye on Sue as they descended.

"You see those mountains over there?" Eric Old Person asked after a while.

"They're gorgeous," Tanya said.

"If it weren't for them, our people might have been forced all the way into the Pacific Ocean by the early Americans," he said. "For this reason, we consider the Badger-Two Medicine our last refuge."

"That's why it's so important to us that all drilling be outlawed here," Terry Murray added.

"You wouldn't put an oil rig in the Sistine Chapel, would you?" Jack asked.

"I suppose not," Sue agreed.

"This is our Sistine Chapel," Jack said.

Tanya pointed to a gravelly cliff edge. "Should I grab these stones?"

"Those will do just fine," the chief said. "If you feel called to them."

"I actually do," Tanya said with a tinge of excitement in her voice.

Ellen and her friends each took handfuls of golf-ball-sized rocks and put them into their bundles before continuing down the slope toward the river.

"We want to be as close to the river as possible," Terry Murray said as he followed his chief.

"That makes sense," Sue said. "I suppose it would be convenient, in case the sweat lodge dehydrates you."

"We do it because the Creator said to do it," the chief said.

They gathered the stones, the sage, and the branches over the course of an hour. Eric Old Person started a campfire with logs that Terry Murray had gathered while Jack Stone and Terry bent the branches and helped Ellen and her friends to tie up the frame with the lengths of rope. Ellen was hot, sweaty, and exhausted, and her friends looked the same. She wished she had water but had been told it would break the required fast.

"It's not very tall, is it," Sue said of the frame, which stood about four feet high and ten feet in diameter when it was finished.

"Do you notice anything about its shape?" the chief asked.

"It reminds me of an Igloo," Tanya said.

"It's meant to be a womb," Jack said.

"When you enter from the east," the chief explained, "you are entering the womb of Mother Earth."

"And when you leave, once it's over," Terry Murray added, "you are reborn."

CHAPTER FOUR

# The Sweat Lodge

E ric Old Person asked Ellen and her friends to add the stones they'd collected to the fire he'd built next to the sweat lodge frame. Then he told them to sprinkle the sage leaves onto the ground beneath the frame. Once they'd finished these tasks, Jack Stone and Terry Murray covered the frame with the skins and blankets— except one blanket, which Jack spread onto the ground outside of the sweat lodge.

"Before we go inside," the chief said, "should you need to break your fast by drinking water, drink this." He held up his canteen. "It's medicine water. We make it with herbs to help purify your system."

Ellen licked her parched lips. "May I have some now?"

"I need some, too," Tanya said.

As the chief passed around the canteens, he said, "If at any time you get too hot in there, feel free to come outside and sit or lie down on this blanket. Then you can rejoin us when you're ready."

"You're making me nervous," Ellen said, trying to sound light-hearted.

"This isn't easy," Jack warned. "It's hard even for the most seasoned tribal member."

"Well, that didn't help," Sue said in her teasing way to Jack.

The chief was the first to climb into the sweat lodge carrying his ceremonial pipe and a canteen. He sat on the opposite end of the opening. Ellen followed and sat to the chief's right. It was dark inside, except for the light coming from the small opening, through which the others were still entering. Ellen sat cross-legged as Jack Stone moved between her and Tanya. Tanya sat between Jack and Terry Murray, by the opening. Sue sat between Terry and the chief. Together they formed a tight circle with their knees touching.

A hole had been dug in the center of their circle and offerings of sage, tobacco, and other herbs had been placed into it.

When Terry Murray closed the flap over the entryway, they were in complete darkness. Ellen couldn't see a thing. Even after her eyes had adjusted to the darkness, she could see nothing beyond her own hand, which she held in front of her face.

Ellen suddenly realized the folly of her and her friends. They were in the wilderness with three men they had just met. What a perfect place for a horrendous crime. She shuddered and closed her eyes.

"Before we begin the sweat rounds," the chief said, "we wish to thank the Creator for his wisdom and gifts."

The chief continued to speak in his native tongue before saying, "Now, we will each say a prayer to the Creator. We also call him Sun, or Napi, or Old Man. They are one and the same. Ask a question or make a request before you draw on the pipe. He may answer you through the smoke. Or he may speak to you through the songs of the wind through the grass or the birds in the nearby trees above us. Listen for the Creator's answer. You may hear it in the song we chant."

The chief led the two other men in a guttural song that sounded like crows. The crowing lasted four beats and was followed by another four beats that sounded like the soft cry of wolves. Then the chant repeated.

"Join in, if you can," Jack said in his baritone voice.

Ellen tried. She sang softly so as not to stand out from the other voices: "Ah, yah, yah, yah, awooh, awooh, awooh, awooh, ah, yah, yah, yah, awooh, awooh, awooh, awooh."

Over the chanting, the chief spoke, "My personal prayer to our Creator is this: Will you help these women to settle the evil spirit residing at

Talks to Buffalo Lodge? Will you help your people to use the estate in a way that will enrich the future of the tribe?"

Ellen could hear the chief suck air through the end of the pipe. Then she felt the smoke he exhaled fill the tent around her as the chief joined back in with the chant: "Ah, yah, yah, yah, awooh, awooh, awooh, awooh, ah, yah, yah, yah, awooh, awooh, awooh, awooh."

Then Sue's voice carried through the darkness. "Please help me to become a worthy steward of Talks to Buffalo Lodge."

After a few seconds, Sue coughed and said, "Excuse me," before continuing the chant, "Ah, yah, yah, yah, awooh, awooh, awooh, awooh, ah, yah, yah, yah, awooh, awooh, awooh, awooh."

Terry Murray then prayed for strength followed by Tanya's prayer for world peace.

A moment later, Jack said, "Creator and Mother Earth, please have pity on me and my family. I pray especially for my granddaughter, who, as you know, is still sick. Please help her to fight the cancer growing inside her, so she can live a long and blessed life."

Ellen wondered about the granddaughter and was sorry that she had cancer. Thoughts for her own prayers suddenly left her mind as she worried over his. Then she was brought from those thoughts as the pipe was thrust into her hands.

"Creator and Mother Earth," Ellen began, not sure what would follow. "I ask you to please watch over all of us and our loved ones. Please give us the peace we need to endure the trials of life."

She put the pipe to her lips and drew in the smoke. She avoided breathing it in too deeply, so as not to break out into a coughing fit. The smoke tasted something like the weed she occasionally smoked in college. She wondered if the pipe contained more than tobacco. Would they get high together? She fought the giggles again as she passed the pipe to Eric Old Person.

After they had each had a turn at the pipe, Terry Murray opened the flap, and Ellen was nearly blinded by the flood of sunlight. Once her eyes had adjusted, she saw he was using the forked stick to lift a few of the coals from the campfire outside into the center of the lodge. Then he closed the flap, and they were once again enveloped by darkness. But this time, they were also surrounded by a stifling heat.

Ellen heard a sizzling sound—from water being added to the coals—and the tent filled with steam. The sweet smell of sage, combined with the slight buzz from the pipe, caused Ellen to breathe in slowly and deeply. Her shoulders dropped as some of the tension left her body.

"We will have another round of prayer," the chief said. "This time, you should think of a story that has left you feeling empty or wounded. This prayer will be for healing."

The chief spoke of the death of his wife two years ago, a death he still grieved. He pleaded with the Creator to fill the emptiness left behind by his wife. Ellen was surprised that the chief openly wept.

Sue spoke of her mother. Through tears, Sue talked about the way she and her mother had been more like best friends throughout Sue's life. She asked the Creator to take away the longing she felt for her mother's company.

Terry Murray asked the Creator to help him with his alcohol addiction so that he could be a better father to his sons. Then Tanya asked for help letting go of Tina and Johnny, the children whom she'd fostered over the past year.

Jack spoke again of his granddaughter and of the leukemia that threatened her life. He focused more on the pain it caused his daughter and wife and how hard it was for him to witness it. He echoed Ellen's prayer for peace.

Ellen found it hard to open up about her own pain. She didn't know how she felt about her breakup with Brian. She didn't know if it was really over between them, or if they would find their way back to each other. She didn't know what she wanted from a lover—or if she wanted one at all. She still desperately missed Paul. She felt alone and forgotten and somehow loose with nothing holding her down. This wasn't a feeling of easy liberty but of terror and anxiety.

Finally, she said, "I pray for healing after the loss of my husband." Then, without elaborating, she took another draw from the pipe and rejoined the song.

A warm buzz lifted her. She felt as if her soul were flying to the ceiling of the lodge.

Ellen was again blinded when Terry Murray opened the flap, without interrupting their song, to add more coals to those already resting on the sage and other herbs in the center of their circle. He dropped the flap as medicine water sizzled against the stones and more steam filled the lodge.

The heat was thick, and Ellen was soon drenched with sweat.

"Ah, yah, yah, yah, awooh, awooh, awooh, awooh, ah, yah, yah, yah, awooh, awooh, awooh, awooh."

"Now we will ask the Creator to expunge us of all negativity, to purify our bodies and our souls," the chief said over the continuous chanting. "We pray for the strength to overcome greed, envy, lust, and laziness. We pray for the will to shun all evil. I personally ask the Creator to help me overcome my selfish desire for solitude, so that I may continue to lead the tribe."

Ellen chanted with the others as the chief drew from the pipe and then filled the lodge with his smoke.

"Help me to better control my eating," Sue said. "So that I may live a healthier, longer life."

"Give me the strength to stop drinking," Terry Murray said, when it was his turn.

"Show me how to take better care of the environment," Tanya prayed. "Help me to recycle, to use sustainable resources, and to not waste. Help me with my garden."

"Help me to curb my spending," Jack prayed. "Let me be content with what I have."

When the pipe was passed to Ellen, she struggled with what to say. She had so many shortcomings. Which were worth mentioning? She ran them over in her head, but the smell of the sage and the smoke made her dizzy, and before she knew what she was doing, she was muttering, "Help me to stop feeling sorry for myself. Help me to be a better mother and friend. Help me to stop focusing on my own pain and loneliness so that I can be an instrument of peace for others."

Ellen was soon sobbing. She was crying so hard, and her lips were quivering so badly, that it was difficult for her to draw smoke from the pipe. She managed to take a little of the smoke in before she passed the pipe to Eric Old Person.

The flap opened, and Terry Murray added more coals. The chief poured more water onto them as the flap closed and darkness and thick steam covered her.

"You can go outside at any time, if needed," the chief reminded her. "Are you okay?"

Ellen lost control as her sobs overwhelmed her.

"Ellen?" Tanya asked through the darkness and over the chanting, which hadn't ceased.

"I'm...oh...kay," Ellen said through her sobs. "Or...I...will...be."

She wiped her eyes. Water seemed to be seeping from her eyelids—from every pour in her skin. She felt faint and exhausted but also relaxed and high. She was soaring. Soaring with the crows.

"Ah, yah, yah, yah, awooh, awooh, awooh, awooh, ah, yah, yah, yah, awooh, awooh, awooh, awooh."

They chanted for many minutes. The passage of time was hard to measure for Ellen. There were times when she felt as if she had left the lodge and was walking around in the wilderness beneath the summer sun, or standing before Weeping Wall full of tears, but then she'd feel Jack Stone's knee pressing against hers, and she'd return to her body and to the chanting.

She wasn't sure how long they'd been chanting when the chief said, "We pray for purity and cleansing. We ask to be made worthy to commune with spirits."

Terry Murray began to speak in his native tongue.

When he'd finished, the chief translated: "He said that great evil is made by great pain. Very grave pain controls Crow Woman. Creator has revealed that she is the evil one who dwells at Talks to Buffalo Lodge."

Ellen opened her eyes wide and tried to see her friends' faces in the darkness, but it was impossible.

"Oh, spirits of the other realm," Sue began over the chanting voices.

"Not *of the other realm*," the chief interrupted. "The spirits share our realm. They are here in the animals and the trees, in the grass and in the wind."

"Pardon me," Sue said. "Oh, spirits. Please help us to bring peace to Crow Woman. Please guide us as we attempt to make contact with her over the next few days."

Ellen flinched when Terry Murray began to shout belligerently in his native tongue. He shouted the same string of syllables over and over.

"What is he saying?" Ellen asked the chief in the darkness.

"He says, 'Crow woman is not alone.'"

CHAPTER FIVE

# Talks to Buffalo Lodge

Are you sure you want to do that?" Sue asked Tanya over breakfast in the lodge the next morning. "Rent a car and drive around the park, all by yourself?"

"It seems unlike you," Ellen added. "We know how much you hate driving."

Tanya took a sip of her hot tea. "I'd rather take my chances on the road than at Talks to Buffalo Lodge. I can't believe you're still going."

"Can't you take a taxi?" Sue asked.

"You know I don't like to talk to strangers," she said.

Ellen swallowed down another bite of her pancake. "So, on Tanya's list of fears, talking to strangers trumps driving. Good to know."

Sue chuckled. "Yes. If we are ever in a fix and need her to drive, we can threaten to invite someone she doesn't know."

"It'll be fun," Tanya insisted, ignoring their jokes. "I want to check out more of the hiking trails and the shops. I think I might buy something for Dave and the kids. And there are lots more restaurants to sample. Are you guys sure I can't tempt you to join me?"

"You know me," Sue said. "I want what I want. Besides, my curiosity has always been greater than my fear."

"Which is why we always get into so much trouble," Ellen said with a smile.

Tanya shrugged. "Fine. Have it your way. But don't say I didn't warn you."

"We could never say *that*," Sue said before bursting into laughter.

An hour later, Ellen and Sue took the hotel shuttle back to the tribal headquarters on the Blackfeet Reservation, where they were met outside by a petite woman with dark, shoulder-length hair.

Sue asked, "Are you the tribal *secretary*?"

The woman smiled. "I wear a lot of hats around here. Tribal secretary is one."

"Oh?" Ellen asked. "What other hats do you wear?"

"I'm also the provost of our community college and the public relations representative for the tribe," the woman said.

"You sound like a busy woman," Ellen said.

"It's nice to meet you," Sue offered the woman her hand. "I'm Sue Graham, and this is Ellen Mohr."

"Karen Murray," the woman said as she shook each of their hands.

"Are you related to Terry Murray?" Ellen asked.

"He's my husband."

"Did he tell you about what happened yesterday?" Sue asked.

Karen led them to a black Honda Accord parked in front of the building. "I know about the purification ceremony, if that's what you mean."

"It seems the spirits channeled him to communicate with us," Ellen explained as she climbed into the passenger's seat, while Sue took the backseat.

Karen turned the key in the ignition. "Yes. He told me. But he has no memory of it—only what the chief relayed to him afterward."

"Well, isn't that strange," Sue said as Karen pulled from the parking lot.

Not long after, Karen turned onto a private dirt road that was lined with thick trees. The road stretched for a mile before the dilapidated two-story ranch house, with its peeling gray paint and decrepit, black-shingled roof, came into view. An old chevy pickup, perhaps from the sixties, sat without wheels in the tall grass on one side of the house. Three dead trees—two in the front and one near the back of the house—stuck up from the earth like the black skeletons of giants. After Karen had parked and Ellen had stepped from the car, she was startled by a flock of crows fleeing from the dead branches above them.

The remains of an old wooden fence stood rotting along one side of the house. Even from where Ellen stood, she could see it was crawling with ants. The front wooden stoop wasn't in much better shape. It was covered with dirt and broken glass, presumably from the two broken windowpanes near the front door.

A second-floor balcony looked out from one side of the house. You couldn't see it from the front, but Ellen had walked from one side to the other and had noticed it on the left side, facing east.

"That doesn't look very safe," Ellen muttered, pointing.

"What part of it do you mean?" Sue asked. "None of it looks safe."

"Ladies, please keep in mind that this house was built in 1890 and hasn't been touched since the '70s."

"Oh, it's been touched," Sue said. "Just not by human hands."

"What about vagrants?" Ellen asked.

"They don't stay long," Karen said. "I can promise you that."

"I don't doubt you," Sue said.

"I'm not sure much of the original structure can be salvaged," Ellen said.

"For once, I may have to agree with you," Sue said. "But at least the land is nice. Except for these dead trees, the rest of the acreage looks beautiful."

"There's a creek that runs along the back of the property, too," Karen pointed out. "And from the second story, you will find amazing views of the nearby mountains."

"How nice," Sue said. "As long as the second story doesn't crumble beneath our feet and plunge us to our deaths."

"Shall we go inside and have a look?" Karen asked.

Ellen and Sue exchanged worried glances.

"We may as well," Sue said. "We've come this far. There's no use in giving up now."

Ellen followed Karen and Sue up the wobbly steps to the front stoop and through the unlocked front door. She was pleasantly surprised when she wasn't accosted by the horrible stench that usually resided in abandoned homes. She supposed the broken windows allowed fresh air to circulate.

She was also surprised to see furniture in the front room. An old armoire stood against the back wall, and, in front of it was a broken bench, covered by a thick, cream-white animal fur. After circling around the bench, Ellen saw the head of a buffalo hanging on the other end.

"I've never seen a white buffalo before," Ellen said.

"I didn't even know such things existed," Sue remarked.

"They're very rare," Karen explained.

"Then why has this been left here to rot?" Ellen wondered. "If it's rare, wouldn't it be valuable?"

"Money isn't as important to us as our sacred ways and beliefs," Karen said. "You see, only the person who was chosen by the Creator to kill a white buffalo may keep its hide. It cannot be sold—though it may be passed down to relatives."

"I've never known anyone who didn't value money," Sue said.

"We value it," Karen said, "just not in excess. I don't expect you to understand."

Sue lifted her brows and gave Ellen a look—a look which acknowledged that she'd been burned by the tribal secretary.

"Do you know who killed the white buffalo?" Ellen asked.

"Talks to Buffalo," Karen said. "The same man for whom this house is named. I guess he had no descendants to pass it onto, so, after his wife died, it remained with the estate. Every person who has owned the house since has become the custodian of the skin. If you decide to buy, you will be the next."

"How wonderful," Sue said with a tinge of sarcasm. "I've always wanted a buffalo hide."

Ellen frowned and whispered to Sue, "Control yourself."

Sue ignored Ellen as she strolled to the armoire and opened the cabinet door. No sooner had she pulled the door open than a rattling sound alarmed them and a small critter scurried across the floor.

Sue jumped back with her hand on her heart. "What the hell was that?"

"I think it was a rat," Karen said. "It's to be expected, considering how long this house has been unoccupied."

"Apparently, it *hasn't* been unoccupied," Sue said as she caught her breath.

Karen pointed to the ceiling. "As you can see, the internal structure has held up pretty well over the years."

Ellen wasn't so sure she agreed but followed Karen into the kitchen, which was outfitted like something from the sixties. Lime-green linoleum covered most of the floor, and Formica countertops lay atop broken lower cabinets made of dark oak. There was an old stove and two rusted metal chairs. Karen flipped a switch, which brought a three-foot-long fluorescent tube on the ceiling to life.

"I'm surprised the electricity works," Ellen said.

"It almost looks quaint," Sue said. "Don't you think, Ellen?"

Ellen frowned. "I have a pretty good imagination, but it must not be as good as yours."

"Well, it looked better in the dark," Sue admitted. "Are those rat turds on the counters and floor?"

"I think so," Karen said.

They followed Karen to a dining room, bathroom, and master bedroom before heading up the rickety stairs to the second floor, where they found two more bedrooms and another bath. Each bedroom led to the side balcony, where the views were spectacular.

"You can see Chief Mountain from here," Karen pointed out. "My people consider it to be the center of the earth."

Although other mountains stretched higher up to the sky further in the background, Chief Mountain stood alone in the foreground. Its shape reminded Ellen of an ancient castle built on a high hill. It had a nearly flat peak and long flat face before it swelled outward.

"Wouldn't it be amazing to wake up to this view every morning?" Sue said.

"I don't think I'd ever get tired of it," Ellen agreed.

Before they headed downstairs, Ellen noticed a gaping hole in the ceiling that opened through the roof to the bright sky above.

She pointed to the hole. "This is why the air isn't stale in this place."

"It also explains why the floorboards directly below it have nearly rotted through," Sue added. "Watch your step."

As they descended the stairs, Sue asked, "Is the water turned on? Does it run?"

"Yes, but I don't think the toilets work," Karen said.

The tribal secretary led them back to the kitchen, where she turned on the faucet at the white apron sink. "See?"

"Yep, it works," Sue said.

While Sue asked questions about the plumbing and sewage, Ellen returned to the main room and to the white buffalo skin. Although it was covered by a thick layer of dust and cobwebs, there was something magnificent about it, and she couldn't resist reaching out to touch the fur. No sooner had her skin made contact with it than she felt something like a jolt of electricity pulse up from her hand, up her arm, and to her chest.

She flinched, released the fur, and took several steps back, whispering, "What was that?"

Sue and Karen continued to discuss the details of the house in the next room and hadn't noticed.

Hesitantly, Ellen inched toward the fur and, with a shaky hand, reached out and touched it again. Just like before, she felt a rush of energy surge through her. This time, she held on, curious to know if something more would happen, but nothing did.

When Sue retuned from the kitchen, Ellen said, "Touch this, and tell me what it feels like."

Sue arched a brow. "Why would I want to touch that dirty old thing? It gives me the creeps."

"Just do it," Ellen said, unable to keep the exasperation from her voice.

Sue did as she was told, for once, as Karen entered from the kitchen.

"It's surprisingly soft," Sue said.

"You didn't feel something?" Ellen asked. "Like a jolt of electricity?"

"No. Why? Did you?"

Ellen glanced at Karen, whose brows had lifted with surprise.

"What?" Ellen asked her. "Does it mean something?"

"I'm not sure," Karen said. "But maybe the spirit that dwells in that skin has made a connection with you."

"Do you mean Crow Woman?" Sue asked. "That's the name of the evil spirit who's attached to this house—according to your husband, anyway."

"Not according to my husband. The name came from Creator. In our language, it is Maisto Aakii."

Ellen shuddered. "Well, when I touched it, it didn't *feel* evil." Had evil entered her heart?

"By the way," Karen said, "that was also the name of Talks to Buffalo's wife. They are probably one and the same."

"Really? Do you know anything more about them?" Ellen asked Karen.

"Not a lot. There may be some records on file—marriage and death certificates—if you want to look for them. We have copies of almost everything from the Indian Bureau as far back as 1871. The documents have been scanned and cross-referenced in the tribal database."

"You said Talks to Buffalo and Crow Woman didn't have any descendants," Ellen said. "Is that right?"

"As far as I know. I don't recall reading about any in the documents pertaining to this property. If there were children, however, there would be birth records. The Indian Bureau was pretty strict about documenting everyone."

Sue folded her arms and turned to Karen. "Do you mind if we conduct our investigation tonight and I give you our answer within the next few days?"

"I suppose that's fine," the tribal secretary replied.

"Is that fine with you, Ellen?"

"The sooner the better," Ellen said. "My curiosity has certainly been piqued."

Ellen followed Sue through the front door to the rotten front stoop. Karen, who was the last to exit, had barely stepped over the threshold when the door slammed shut, causing her to utter a soft cry of surprise.

"Was that the wind?" Sue asked.

Ellen gazed at the still, tall grass surrounding the abandoned pickup truck. "I don't think so."

"Definitely not," Karen said. "Are you sure you know what you're doing with this paranormal investigation stuff?"

Sue turned to Ellen, who shrugged.

"We think so," Ellen said.

During the drive back to the tribal headquarters, Karen asked Ellen and Sue how they had become paranormal investigators. They told her about the Gold House in San Antonio and had just finished recounting their experiences in Tulsa with the Monroe Social Club when Karen pulled in the parking lot of the tribal headquarters.

Wanting to hear more, Karen invited them to join her for coffee in her office, where they continued their stories. Karen sat behind her desk, opposite Sue and Ellen, as they told her about the Demon Baby of New Orleans, the Shanghai Tunnels in Portland, and the haunting of Hoover Dam.

"How fascinating," Karen said, when they had finished. "What interesting lives you lead."

Ellen smiled, realizing it was true. So, why was she so mopey all the time?

"And what will tonight's investigation entail?" Karen asked. "Can you tell me about it?"

"Would you care to join us?" Ellen asked her.

"I can't tonight. I have plans. I don't usually on a Friday night, but I do tonight."

"Let us know if you change your mind," Sue said. "You have my number."

"Thanks."

Ellen suddenly had an idea. "Do you think we could take a look at those records you mentioned? I'd like to learn as much as possible about Talks to Buffalo and Crow Woman before we get started tonight."

"That's a good idea," Sue said.

Karen began typing on the keyboard connected to the PC on her desk. "Let's see what I can find."

Ellen and Sue exchanged looks of excitement while they waited for the tribal secretary to conduct her search.

"Hmm. Okay, I did find a marriage certificate for Talks with Buffalo and Crow Woman for June 12th of 1890."

Ellen and Sue climbed to their feet to stand behind Karen, so they could look over her shoulder at the screen. It showed a scanned document that had been crudely typed on plain paper. The document bore a seal that read "U.S. Department of the Interior Bureau of Indian Affairs" with the image of an eagle.

"According to this document, Crow Woman wasn't *Crow*," Karen said. "She was actually *Piegan*. I wonder why they called her *Crow* Woman."

"Can you check for death certificates?" Sue asked.

Karen tapped at her keyboard and pulled up another document.

"Talks with Buffalo died of cirrhosis of the liver in 1932," Karen said. She tapped a few more keys and pulled up another document. "And, let's see, Crow Woman died in 1943 of dehydration and malnutrition."

"How terrible!" Ellen said. "How old was she?"

"Seventy," Karen said. "It wasn't uncommon back then. Many Blackfeet died that way."

"How sad," Sue said.

"Let me look for birth records under their names," Karen said as she typed at her keyboard.

She clicked on a hyperlink and brought up a birth certificate.

"A boy," she said. "Born to Talks to Buffalo and Crow Woman on September 20, 1891. Here he's only called First Son. That's not uncommon, as some families like to name their children later, according to their personality or traits."

"But they did have a child," Sue said.

"Yes. Now I'm searching through our census data. Ah, here it is. Aisaistowa Iini, or Talks to Buffalo, Maisto Aakii, or Crow Woman, and A'atsista, or Rabbit. There are no other children listed as of 1908."

"Can you find anything else about Rabbit?" Ellen asked.

"Let me check for a death certificate for A'atsista Aisaistowa Iini," Karen said as she tapped at her keyboard. "Hmm. Nothing."

"Does that mean he's still alive?" Ellen wondered.

"Not necessarily," Karen said. "Besides, that would make him around 130 years old. He probably left the reservation sometime before he died. Wait, let me check something else."

Ellen held her breath as Karen conducted another search.

"Okay, here's something," Karen said. "In 1900, A'atsista Aisaistowa Iini, or Rabbit Talks to Buffalo, was enrolled in a boarding school."

"Does it say which school?" Sue asked.

"No, but I know where he would have been taken," Karen said. "Holy Family Mission. Back then, nearly all the Blackfeet children were forced to attend Holy Family as part of the U.S. government's effort to train the Indian out of them. Children were ripped from their parents' arms, bussed from their homes, and only permitted to visit a few times a year, if at all."

"Dear God," Sue mumbled.

"But what happened to Rabbit after he went to school?" Ellen asked.

"The bureau might have records. And, although the boarding school closed decades ago, Holy Family Mission Church still holds mass every Sunday. They may have records, too. It's only about a half-hour away."

"And where's the bureau?" Sue asked.

"Right around the corner," Karen said.


Ellen and Sue met Tanya for a late lunch a few minutes away from their hotel at a place called Rock-N-Roll Bakery: Gear and Goodness.

"I read about their vegetable quiche and cinnamon rolls online," Sue said as they followed the hostess to a table, where they were surrounded by mountain views. "The pies are supposed to be good, too."

"I may need to fast again after this meal," Ellen said, looking over the menu. "Everything sounds delicious."

"Smells delicious, too," Tanya said.

After they had ordered, Sue and Ellen told Tanya about their morning touring the property and searching the records of the tribe, the bureau, and the Holy Family Mission.

"You should have called me," Tanya said. "I would have met you. I spent most of the morning in the Glacier Park Lodge gift shop."

"What about your hiking and shopping at the park?" Sue asked.

"After I got the rental, I chickened out. I hated not knowing my way around. So, I went back and walked around the lodge."

"We should have called," Ellen agreed. "I'm sorry we didn't."

"Oh, well," Tanya said just as the waitress arrived with their quiche.

"Let me know if I can get you anything else," their waitress said before leaving their table.

Ellen took a bite and sighed with pleasure.

"Hmm," Sue said. "This is delicious."

"Mm-hmm," Tanya agreed.

"So, I was about to explain that, while we haven't made much progress yet," Ellen said before taking a sip of her tea, "we met someone who seems eager to help."

"Oh?' Tanya asked. "Who?"

"A Jesuit priest named Father Gonzales," Ellen replied. "He's very interested in the history of Holy Family and says he'd be delighted to conduct some research for us."

"Let's hope he unearths something useful," Sue said. "And now for the more important question of the day: what should I order to go, for later tonight? Cinnamon rolls or a cherry pie?"

CHAPTER SIX

# A Paranormal Investigation

While Sue took initial readings downstairs at Talks to Buffalo Lodge, Ellen set up a full-spectrum camera in one of the upstairs bedrooms, which had grown dark with the setting sun, as all the bulbs in the upstairs light fixtures were dead. She had just found the right camera angle to capture both the room and the hallway when she tripped and fell on her hands and knees, and her cell phone slipped from her pants pocket.

"Ow," she muttered beneath her breath.

She grabbed her phone and climbed to her feet—something that was getting harder and harder to do with each passing year.

Her hands were covered in dirt and splinters from the old wooden floors. She glanced around to see what could have caused her to trip. There were no cords—the camera ran on a battery. Finding nothing, she went to the bathroom down the hall to wash her hands and to remove the splinters. She was removing the last of them when the bathroom door suddenly slammed shut.

"Sue?" Ellen called, wondering how her friend could be in the hallway without Ellen having heard the old floorboards creak.

When Sue didn't reply, Ellen attempted to open the door, but it wouldn't budge. She turned the lock on the knob, but it did no good. She pushed the lock the other way and still had no luck. Then Ellen threw her body against the door, to no avail.

"Sue?" she called again, this time with a hint of panic in her voice. "Sue? Can you hear me?"

When Sue didn't reply, Ellen took out her phone with the intent of calling her friend but found she had no cell service.

"Just great," she muttered. Then, at the top of her voice, she shrieked, "Sue!"

She heard her friend call out from below, "What's wrong?"

"I'm stuck inside the bathroom! Can you help me, please?"

"I was hoping to avoid the stairs, Ellen! Did you try the lock?"

Beneath her breath, Ellen muttered, "Unbelievable." Aloud she said, "I hadn't thought of that!"

"Are you still stuck then?"

"Sue! I'm locked in. Get up here! Now!"

"Okay, okay! Hold your horses!"

Ellen fumed and tapped her foot impatiently while she listened to the sound of the rickety steps beneath Sue's weight. Ellen glanced in the cracked mirror above the sink and had a shock when she saw Weeping Wall reflected there.

Finally, the doorknob rattled.

"See what I mean?" Ellen said. "It's not locked, but it won't open."

The knob rattled again.

"Sue, I don't think that's doing any good. We may need to call someone. Do you have any cell phone service?"

The knob rattled again, and this time the door burst open.

Relieved, Ellen stepped from the hallway only to find it empty.

"Sue?"

"I said hold your horses! I'm coming!" Sue called from the first floor.

The hair on the back of Ellen's neck stood on end as a chill ran down her spine. She quickly made her way to the stairs and met Sue on the ground-floor landing.

"Oh, good," Sue said. "I didn't need this after all."

She held up an old wire coat hanger that she had twisted apart.

"I thought I'd have to pick the lock, but you got out on your own. How?"

Ellen could barely breathe as she recounted what had happened.

"Oh, boy," Sue said. "We've got our work cut out for us, don't we? Let's hurry up and make our circle of protection."

Ellen found the cannister of salt in her bag and began pouring it in a wide circle around them and the two metal chairs they'd brought into the main room from the kitchen. As with the upstairs, the bulbs in the light fixtures overhead were dead, save for the fluorescent tube in the kitchen, which, together with the moonlight pouring in from the front windows, afforded enough light to see by, though just barely.

"We should have asked Tom to come," Ellen said as she poured.

Sue lit candles at each of the cardinal points along their circle. "Heavens no. He would have spoiled all the fun."

"What were we thinking? Two old women alone in an old house full of evil and, apparently, without cell phone service."

"Old women? Speak for yourself. And surely Tanya would come out and check on us if we didn't return to our rooms tonight."

Ellen rolled her eyes. "I'm sure. The only one of the three of us who falls asleep before nine PM will notice if we don't make it back."

Sue inspected her phone. "You're right about having no service. I guess that's something we should have checked earlier."

"You think?"

"Are you saying we should quit?" Sue asked. "Pack everything back up into the rental and give up?"

Ellen sighed. "No. We've come this far. We may as well keep going."

"It's a good thing I brought along the cherry pie and cinnamon rolls," Sue said with a laugh. "We can always stress-eat our way through the night."

Ellen's feelings of panic eased up a bit as Sue continued to laugh.

"We can do this," Ellen said—more to herself than to Sue.

"Of course, we can." Sue sat in one of the two metal chairs, cautiously at first, to make sure it would hold. When it did, she asked, "Ready?"

Ellen glanced around the room. The bakery boxes and bottled water lay on the floor at Sue's feet. One of the full-spectrum cameras stood near the front of the house directed at them. There was another in the kitchen and a third in the master bedroom, in addition to the one upstairs. Ellen couldn't remember if she had turned on the upstairs camera but wasn't about to leave the circle now.

"You plugged in the electromagnetic pump?" Ellen asked.

"Don't worry," Sue said. "My phone has died enough times during these investigations to help me to remember to do that."

"What about the motion detectors?" Ellen asked.

"All on and ready to go."

Ellen grabbed a handheld EMF detector from the bag near her feet as she sat in the chair opposite Sue with the boxed bakery goods on the floor between them. "What kind of initial readings did you get?"

"The EMF detector went crazy in just about every room downstairs, especially around that ghastly buffalo fur. But the temperature was consistent, at seventy degrees. Did you get anything upstairs?"

"No, but that's okay. Let's get started."

"Oh, spirits of the other," Sue stopped short—probably remembering what the chief had said about the spirits dwelling in *this* realm. "Ahem. Oh, spirits, if you can hear me, please know that we come in peace. We're here to help you to find peace, if we can. Please look for the light of our candles and follow the smells of our baked goods. Draw energy from our electromagnetic pump. If anyone can hear me, please use that energy to give us a sign, like a knock or something."

Ellen glanced around the room, not expecting anything to happen, since it usually took a while for the spirits to be coaxed into cooperating. She was utterly shocked when there came, not one, but a flood of knocks all over the house, as if multiple spirits were knocking on every square inch of the walls, ceilings, and floors!

Sue looked at her with frightened eyes.

The flames on two of the candles went out.

Ellen clutched the *gris gris* bag that hung from a leather strap around her neck and whispered, "What have we gotten ourselves into?"

With quivering lips and wide eyes, Sue said, "Thank you, spirits. We receive your sign with gratitude. You can stop now."

The knocks did not cease.

"Oh, boy," Ellen muttered.

"Dear spirits," Sue began, over the horrendous and terrifying knocking. "We'd like to talk with you, if you'd allow it. If you are willing to talk with us, please knock once for no and two for yes."

The knocking ceased.

Ellen sighed with relief.

Sue took a deep breath and repeated, "If you're willing to talk with us, please knock once for no and two for yes."

One loud knock resounded through the abandoned house from somewhere upstairs.

"That seems pretty clear," Ellen said. "She, or they, don't want to talk to us."

Sue frowned. "Why don't we try the Ouija Board? Maybe we'll have better luck."

Ellen's hands were trembling as she pulled the board and planchette from the duffle bag at her feet. Then she scooted her chair closer to Sue's, so that their knees touched, and she lay the board across their knees before setting the plastic planchette on the center of it. She and Sue lightly placed their fingertips on the planchette. Sue's fingers were trembling, too.

"Let me try," Ellen whispered.

Sue nodded.

"If anyone is here, and if you wish to communicate with us, please use this board to give us your message." Ellen moved the planchette around as she said, "To answer yes, move the indicator this way. For no, move it here. You can also use these letters and numbers to spell things out."

Without Ellen having to say more, the planchette began to move, apparently of its own accord.

Quickly, the planchette moved to M-I-N-A-T-S-I-P-O-Y-I-T.

Then it came to a stop.

Sue tried to pronounce it. "Minatsipoyit? Is that your name?"

The indicator flew across the board to S-A-A.

Ellen looked up at Sue with bent brows, but before she could say anything, the planchette moved again to the same letters as before: M-I-N-A-T-S-I-P-O-Y-I-T.

"Let's assume that's her—or his—name," Ellen said. Then she added, "Thank you, Minatsipoyit. Could you please use the planchette to tell us the year of your birth?"

Once again, the planchette quickly glided over the board, so fast, that both women found it hard to keep their fingertips on it, as it spelled: M-I-N-A-T-S-I-P-O-Y-I-T.

"This isn't getting us anywhere," Sue whispered. "Maybe the spirit can't speak English."

"I have an idea." Ellen set the Ouija board aside and rummaged through her duffle bag for her sketch pad and pencil. She'd been wanting to try something new ever since the horned owl, or the spirit possessing it, had channeled her to draw the Boulder City Hospital with the X beneath the mesquite trees. Ellen had watched Miss Margaret Myrtle work in a similar way during their investigation in Tulsa.

"Show me." Ellen gently traced the pencil back and forth over the paper. She closed her eyes, and, again, she said, "Show me."

Ellen tried to open her mind to any spirits wishing to channel her. She softly traced her pencil back and forth across the paper, waiting for someone to take over.

After a few minutes of silence—save for the soft scratch of her lead on paper—Sue said, "Um, Ellen. You might want to open your eyes."

Ellen looked at her sketch pad but was disappointed to find nothing more than a series of horizontal lines.

She glanced up at Sue, who was holding very still and looking over Ellen's shoulder.

Ellen turned her head and gasped. Floating in the air behind her at eye level were two rusty nails, a rock the size of a lemon, a bent spoon, a broken brick, and the wire coat hanger Sue had untwisted earlier.

"What the heck?" Ellen muttered.

"While you were drawing, they flew like lightning from different parts of the house toward the back of your head and stopped when they reached the circle of protection."

Ellen's mouth went dry at the realization that something hostile had tried to attack her.

"What do we do now?" Ellen asked Sue.

"I can tell you what we *don't* do. We don't leave this circle until help arrives."

"What help?" Ellen said. "Tanya won't come. Not until the morning, anyway, when we don't show up for breakfast."

"I'm not about to leave this circle, Ellen. Are you?"

Ellen glanced back again at the objects hanging ominously in midair on the outskirts of their circle.

"We could make a run for it—leave all the equipment and make a beeline for the rental car."

"Very funny. You know I can't run."

Ellen climbed to her feet with the intent of persuading Sue to leave, but when the floating objects flew around the circle of protection and tried, once again, to attack her, she sat back down.

"I suppose we can wait a little while longer, at least until the spirit calms down."

# CHAPTER SEVEN

# Lost

E llen was startled by the sound of a car door slamming shut. She blinked against the sunlight flooding in through the front windows and discovered she'd fallen asleep on the floor in Talks to Buffalo Lodge between her duffle bag and the boxes of baked goods. The objects that had been floating in the air all night lay strewn on the floor outside the circle of protection. The flames on the last remaining candles had burned out. Sue snored in the metal chair with her chin on her chest.

"Sue? Ellen?"

"Tanya?" Ellen shouted. She heard a car driving away. "Tanya? Are you out there?"

"Yes. It's me!" Tanya cried. "Are you guys okay?"

Tanya pushed open the front door, and more of the morning light flooded the room.

Ellen flinched when the objects that had previously been floating lifted into the air before flying across the room at lightning speed toward Tanya.

"Run!" Ellen screamed.

With a shriek, Tanya disappeared from the doorway.

"What?" Sue shouted as she opened her eyes. "What's happening?"

"Tanya?" Ellen shouted. "Are you okay?"

"What's going on?" Sue asked again.

"Tanya came for us, but the ghost attacked her with those same things it hurled at me last night."

"Is Tanya alright?"

"I don't know. Should we leave the circle and find out?"

Sue rubbed her eyes. "Well, she could be bleeding to death."

"I'll go," Ellen offered. "You stay, just in case it's not safe."

"Well, if you insist."

Ellen stood up and crept to the edge of their circle of protection. Her heart raced as she prepared to run. She took a deep breath and sprinted as quickly as she could through the front door.

Once outside, she glanced around for Tanya and found her sitting in the front passenger's seat of the rental car with her hands over her face. The window beside her was broken. The front left tire had a rusty nail stuck into it.

Ellen ran across the dirt and patches of tall grass to the car. "Tanya?"

She lifted her face. "Let's get the heck out of here. Where's Sue?"

"I'll go get her. You wait here."

Ellen sprinted across the yard and through the front door, where an old book smacked her in the head before crashing to the floor.

"Hurry!" she cried to Sue, ignoring the pain on her forehead.

Sue scooped up the bakery boxes and bottled water.

"Leave those!" Ellen said. "Just come on!"

Without taking Ellen's advice, Sue carried the boxes and bottles as she floundered from the circle, uttering a low, "Ahhhh," of terror. Then she scrambled through the door with Ellen.

Ellen climbed behind the wheel as Sue clamored into the back. But when Ellen pushed the button on the ignition, nothing happened.

"Why isn't is starting?" Ellen shouted anxiously.

"Do you have the key up there?" Sue asked. "It has to be close, or the button won't work."

"Yes, it's in my pocket." Ellen dug it out and tried the button again. Nothing. She tried again and again and still…nothing.

"Do you think the ghost drained the battery?" Tanya asked.

"Oh, God." Ellen folded her arms over the steering wheel and dropped her head with frustration.

"I should have asked the shuttle driver to wait," Tanya said. "He had other passengers to drop off, and I wasn't thinking."

"You couldn't have known," Ellen said.

"Do you have cell service, Tanya?" Sue asked from the back before she guzzled down some water.

Tanya took out her phone. "No bars." She tapped at her phone. "No. No service. Damn!"

"We're only a couple of miles away from the nearest house," Ellen said. "Sue, you can wait here, if you want, while Tanya and I go for help."

"Why don't you stay with me, Ellen, and let Tanya go for help?"

"I don't want to go by myself," Tanya said.

"Well, I don't want to wait here by myself. You stay with me and let Ellen go."

"There's no way I'm staying here," Tanya said.

"Come with us," Ellen said to Sue.

Sue pushed her dark bangs from her eyes. "I'll just slow you down, but I guess there's little choice."

The three set off toward the main road. They each carried a water bottle, and Tanya had her purse. Sue and Ellen had abandoned theirs at the house, but they each had their phones, even if they were dead. Tanya kept checking hers for service.

The canopy created by the thick trees lining the dirt road blocked much of the sunlight, making it appear later than it really was. Ellen was grateful for the shade and for the cool breeze. In San Antonio, it was probably in the late nineties; but here, it felt like it was sixty degrees.

"So, what happened last night?" Tanya asked. "Why didn't you come back to the lodge?"

Ellen recounted what had happened, with a few interjections from Sue. The two of them huffed and puffed, despite their slow pace. Only Tanya seemed able to breathe properly.

"Minatsipoyit?' Tanya repeated, when they'd finished their story. "I wonder what that means."

"I suppose we can ask one of the members of the tribe," Sue said.

They trudged along in silence. The dirt road seemed to stretch on forever.

After a while, Ellen said, "Didn't it seem as if the spirit wanted us out of there?"

Sue laughed. "That's an understatement."

"Then why drain our car battery?" Ellen asked. "Why not make it easier for us to get away?"

"Because the ghost is pure evil," Tanya replied. "Don't try to use logic to understand pure evil."

"I don't believe in pure evil," Ellen said. "Remember what the chief said? He said that great evil is made by great pain. Whatever spirit is tormenting us is doing so because of its own torment."

"Maybe the ghost had nothing to do with the car not starting," Sue said.

They continued on in silence. Many minutes passed. Sue's pace slackened. Ellen thought that perhaps an entire hour had gone by since they'd first set foot toward the main road.

"We should be to the road by now," she said. "Didn't Karen say it was only a mile?"

"I believe so," Sue said. "But maybe she was mistaken."

"We've walked more than a mile," Tanya said. "I walk two miles nearly every day, and this feels longer than my usual route."

"Maybe it's because I'm slowing you down," Sue offered.

"No, that's not it," Tanya assured her.

Up ahead, a flock of over thirty crows flew from the canopy onto the dirt road, about twenty yards away.

"What's this?" Tanya muttered as she slowed her pace.

Sue stopped in her tracks. "Why are they staring at us?"

"They aren't staring at us," Ellen scoffed, but Sue was right. Ellen took a few steps forward and froze.

"Yes, they are," Tanya said. "Maybe we should turn around."

"They're giving me the creeps," Sue whispered. "It's like they want to eat us."

Ellen shuddered. "Ugh. Don't say that."

Tanya backed away from the birds. "This doesn't seem natural."

"I shouldn't have left the circle of protection," Sue said.

"You should have brought the salt out with you instead of the pie and cinnamon rolls," Ellen complained.

"Cinnamon *roll*," Sue corrected. "I ate the rest last night and thought one of you might like the last one. I was trying to be thoughtful."

"Oh, what do we do?" Tanya whispered.

Suddenly the flock lifted from the dirt path and flew directly toward them. Ellen and her friends screamed and scattered.

Ellen pushed through the trees and brush and into the surrounding woods, flapping her arms to shoo away the birds. She felt one of them in her hair, causing her to shriek and blindly swat the air overhead as she went wildly forward, getting scratched by the thorny underbrush along the way. A thick gnarly root snagged her foot, and she stumbled to the ground, hurting her ankle in the fall. When she tried to stand up, she winced with pain. Her ankle could not bear the weight. She fell back onto her bottom onto a patch of cool dirt.

At least the birds had gone. But where were Sue and Tanya?

"Sue?" she cried. "Tanya?"

When they didn't answer, she shouted again. She continued to cry out for them until her throat hurt. She glanced around for the water bottle she'd dropped during her scare with the birds but didn't see it.

"Damn," she muttered.

Her lips were parched, and her throat was sore, and she could really use a drink. She sat there for a few minutes as tears pricked her eyes. Then she tried once again to climb to her feet, thinking she couldn't be that far from the dirt road. Sue and Tanya would have an easier time finding her if she could make it out of the woods and into the open.

She winced as she staggered a few feet in the direction she had come.

"Nope," she muttered. "You're not going anywhere in this state."

As she fell back to the ground, she lost her balance, rolled onto her back, and struck her head on a rock, knocking her out cold.

Ellen blinked and rubbed her head. How long had she been out? Dusk had fallen and, together with the thick canopy overhead, had diminished the visibility in the woods.

"Sue?" Ellen cried out. "Tanya?"

She climbed to her feet and winced at the pain in her ankle. It had swelled the size of an orange.

"Geez," she muttered. "I hope it's not broken."

She hobbled through the brush, in spite of the severe pain, in the direction she believed was the dirt road—however, nothing looked familiar in the growing darkness, and she wasn't sure if, in her fall, she'd gotten turned around.

After many minutes had passed, Ellen wondered if she'd been going the wrong way. Without the sun, it was difficult to tell. She leaned against the trunk of a tree and sighed. Tears of frustration welled in her eyes.

"Anyone there?" she cried. "Can someone help me?"

A twig snapped in the distance.

"Tanya?" she shouted. "Sue?"

Brush rustled but not from the wind. Something was in the woods with her, and it was getting closer.

"Tanya? Is that you?"

Ellen began to tremble. Could it be a bear?

She backed away from the sound of snapping twigs and rustling brush. Her heart pounded against her ribs. She could barely feel the pain in her ankle as she held her breath and scrambled through the woods. Where was that damn dirt road? She tried her best to pick up her speed, but the thing in the woods quickened its pace, too.

Panting now from fear and pain, she stubbed the toes of her good foot against a rock, and down she went with a cry. Before she could clamor to her feet again, something emerged from the brush and stood over her, just a few feet away.

It was a white buffalo, and it was glowing.

"Help me," the buffalo said.

Ellen lifted her brows, realizing it wasn't an animal, but a man—or the ghost of a young man.

"Who are you?" she asked.

"I've gone by many names. My father and mother called me Rabbit, because one of my legs was longer than the other, and whenever I walked, I appeared to hop. The teachers at Holy Family Mission called me Randal Smith."

"Was your father called Talks to Buffalo and your mother called Crow Woman?"

The beast nodded.

"Were either of them also called Minatsipoyit?" Ellen asked.

"No. Why?"

Ellen shook her head, wondering if there were someone other than the Crow Woman haunting Talks to Buffalo Lodge. "Never mind. Why do you need my help?"

"My body is lost," he said. "My mother won't find peace until it's found. And she wants justice—or vengeance."

"Where is it? How did you die?"

"I don't know. I can't remember much. I think I was strangled."

Ellen's mouth dropped open. "By whom?"

"I don't know. But it happened at school, in my twelfth grade."

"Holy Family Mission?"

The beast nodded. "My mother won't rest. She's angry—angry that I was taken from her, angry that I was murdered, angry that my killer got away with it, and angry that she didn't know any of this until she died and found me trapped in the buffalo skin. Can you help me?"

Ellen licked her dry lips. "I think your mother tried to kill me and my friends. Or is there someone there with her at the house?"

"She hates white people. She doesn't trust you."

Ellen supposed she didn't blame her. "Can't you convince her to trust us? It would make it easier for me to help you."

"I don't think so. When you return to the house, take one of the Blackfeet with you. That might make a difference."

Ellen sucked in her lips and nodded.

"There's something else," the white buffalo said.

"I'm listening."

"I can feel the white buffalo pulling toward another. It belongs to someone else now. I don't know who. I thought, when you touched it, that it belonged to you. It responded to you. Did you feel it?"

Ellen nodded.

"Maybe you are meant to find its rightful owner. Maybe, if you can find my body, the buffalo will lead you to him. I'm not sure if I can leave until you do."

Finding the hide's rightful owner seemed impossible to Ellen. Where would she start? "I'll try my best. But for now, can you help me? I'm lost, and I have a hurt ankle."

"I already have," he said.

She furrowed her brows and looked around.

"Open your eyes," he said.

"Huh?"

"Ellen, open your eyes!"

With a gasp, Ellen blinked to find Tanya and Sue bending over her, where she lay on the ground in the woods.

"Thank God!" Tanya cried. "I thought you were dead!"

Ellen carefully sat up. Light filtered through the trees. Her head throbbed. "Not dead, but I think I've broken my ankle. How long was I out?"

"That depends on how long ago you passed out," Sue said. "We've been searching for you for over an hour."

"Only an hour? It seemed longer. How did you find me?"

Sue and Tanya exchanged enigmatic looks.

"What?" Ellen asked.

"This is going to sound strange," Sue said. "But, well, we thought we saw a white buffalo, and this is where it led us."

"Then it disappeared," Tanya said. "Strange, right?"

Ellen's mouth fell open as she remembered her dream. "Yes, but I believe you. I think it visited me in a dream."

Tanya offered a hand to Ellen. "Come on. Let's get out of here."

Ellen groaned from the pain in her head and her ankle. Once she was on her feet, her friends each wrapped an arm around her waist to help her along.

"Do you know the way?" she asked them.

"The road is just over there," Sue said. "We were closer to the main road than we thought. Tanya and I could hear cars on the road as we were looking for you."

"That's good news."

As they hobbled through the brush, Ellen told them what Rabbit told her in her dream.

"But if he died at Holy Family Mission, wouldn't he have been found and buried by now?" Tanya asked.

"Obviously not," Sue said, "yet that's a long time for a body to have gone undetected. I'm not sure where to begin to look for him."

They stepped from the woods and onto the dirt road.

"Thank God," Ellen said. "Which way do we go now?"

"Hmm. Don't we want to go right?" Sue asked.

"No, I thought left," Tanya said.

Ellen sighed. "Great."

Just then, the wind whipped their hair back. Ellen almost fell, but her friends caught her just as a white buffalo whirled past them on the road and then disappeared.

"You must be right," Sue said to Tanya. "We should go left, if we're to believe the white buffalo."

They trod along the dirt path for another five minutes, when the paved road, at long last, came into view.

Even better, a car was pulled over on the side of the road, and the driver was bent over a phone.

As they neared the car, Ellen recognized the black Honda Accord that belonged to Karen Murray.

"Karen?" Ellen shouted as they approached the vehicle.

A window rolled down to reveal, not Karen, but Terry Murray.

"What in the world?" he said. "How did you ladies end up *here*?"

"We could ask the same of you," Sue said. "But we won't, because you're a sight for sore eyes, if there ever was one."

# CHAPTER EIGHT

# The Jesuit Priest

S omeone else better drive," Terry Murray said after Ellen and her friends had asked for a lift. "I thought I was sober enough, but I nearly hit a tree early this morning. I've been sitting here, rather stunned, ever since."

"I'll drive," Sue offered as she helped Ellen into the backseat.

Terry climbed in behind the driver's seat beside Ellen.

"It's good you had the sense to pull over," Ellen said. "Have you thought about getting professional help?"

Tanya climbed into the front passenger's seat as Sue went around and got behind the wheel.

"I have help, for all the good it's done me."

"Is there something else the matter, Terry?" Ellen asked as she strapped herself in.

"I won't bother you with my troubles." He burst into tears. "Karen left me last night. We were at the casino, for a date night, trying to patch things up, and, like always, I drank too much. She told me not to come home. Then she got a ride and left me there."

"Oh, no," Ellen said. "I'm so sorry."

Tanya glanced back and frowned but said nothing.

Sue started the engine. Ellen was relieved when the car came to life.

"Where should we go first?" Sue asked.

"Better drop me at my sister's house," he said. "I'm sure she won't mind giving you a ride. Take this road for another mile and then turn left."

Sue pulled off, and they sat in awkward silence for a while.

Then Ellen asked Terry, "By any chance, do you know what Minatsipoyit means?"

"Stop talking," he said.

Ellen blushed. "Oh, I'm sorry."

"That's what it means," he said. "*Mina tsipoyit.* It means *stop talking.*"

Ellen spent the next several days in her room at Glacier Park Lodge with her ankle on ice. She'd seen a doctor and had discovered that it wasn't broken, just sprained, and had been told to stay off it for at least a week, or until the tenderness went away. So, she spent her days on pain medication watching Netflix while Sue and Tanya visited the casino, the shops, and the restaurants.

Although Sue had gone back with Karen Murray to Talks to Buffalo Lodge to retrieve their purses and anything else she could carry, and she'd had the rental towed back to the rental place, they'd decided to leave the heavier equipment until Ellen could return to help with another investigation, if they could convince Karen Murray to accompany them.

Ellen was about to begin another episode of *Downton Abbey* when her phone rang.

Not recognizing the number, she said, "Hello?"

"Hello, Mrs. Mohr?"

"Yes?"

"This is Father Gonzales, from Holy Family Mission Church."

"Hello, Father. Thanks so much for getting back to me."

"I'm sorry it's taken so long, but I think you'll be interested in what I've discovered."

Ellen sat up in her chair. "Really? What is it?"

"I think you'd better come for a visit. It's a story better told in person."

Ellen sighed. "Unfortunately, I've sprained my ankle. Is there any chance you'd be willing to come visit me at Glacier Park Lodge?"

"I could come in an hour, if that's convenient."

Ellen smiled. "That would be great. My friends should be back by then. Call when you arrive, and we'll meet you in the lobby."

An hour later, Ellen and her friends sat with Father Gonzales in the great lobby of Glacier Park Lodge, with its forty-foot pine posts and colorfully upholstered rustic furniture. They each sipped cups of coffee as Father Gonzales reported his findings.

The Jesuit priest was an attractive young man in his mid-thirties with short brown hair and round, dark eyes. His lips were thick, and he spoke with a Spanish accent. Ellen suspected, without asking, that he was originally from Central America.

He sat on the edge of his seat, leaning with his elbows on his knees, and spoke with an animated demeanor.

"Before I share the details of what I've learned," he began, after introductions and small talk had been made, "I want to explain something about Holy Family Mission." He cleared his throat. "We know *now* that the goals of the boarding school in the late 1800s and early 1900s were wrong. Mostly Western European Jesuit priests and Ursuline nuns—not to mention the American pioneers—were horrified by the polygamy and pagan sun worship of the Native Americans. It was thought to be uncivilized and a barrier to eternal salvation."

"But not anymore?" Sue asked.

Father Gonzales blushed. "Well, morally speaking, we still don't approve of polygamy and paganism, but we've also learned to respect cultural customs that are different from our own. You see, back then, the goal was to stifle the Indian to save the soul. The priests and nuns emphatically believed in their work. They felt they had the precious souls of the Indian children in their hands—that they were responsible for them. And they made great sacrifices to answer the calling to save the children."

"What sacrifices?" Ellen wanted to know.

"Have you ever visited Montana at any other time of year?" he asked.

The three women shook their heads.

"The climate is brutal. Summer lasts for the blink of an eye, and it goes straight to winter, with no spring to speak of. Farming in such conditions in those days was all but futile, and food was scarce. The men and women who served often died on the job—from starvation, frostbite, hostile Indians, or exhaustion. People today seem to imagine a bunch of haughty, power-hungry priests and nuns that enjoyed controlling their victims, when, in fact, they served at great costs to their personal well-being."

"I doubt they suffered more than the native children and their families," Tanya muttered.

"I don't doubt you're right," Father Gonzales said. "Suffering that was made worse by the goals of the U.S. government."

"In what way?" Sue asked.

"Well, you see, while the priests and nuns wanted to save the soul of every man, woman, and child, the federal government wanted to make the tribes docile and easy to control, through the indoctrination and assimilation of their children. The church couldn't have done it without federal funding."

"Forgive me, Father," Ellen began, "but what's your point in telling us this?"

Father Gonzales clasped his hands together. "I stumbled upon an interesting document from 1909 regarding Randal Smith—er, Rabbit. It declared him missing and presumed dead."

Ellen's brows shot up. "Why didn't you say?"

"Because there's more to it," he said. "You see, this puzzled me, especially when I found no mention of it in any of the newspaper records online."

"So, what do you think happened?" Sue asked as she glanced excitedly at Ellen and Tanya.

"I decided to comb through the books of letters that have been left behind by the Jesuit priests and brothers who've served at Holy Family Mission over the years. I focused on those written in 1908 and 1909 and found the diaries of three different priests. I read through them and was shocked by what I uncovered in one of them—in the letters of Father Jerome Galdas."

"Well, don't leave us hanging," Sue said. "What was it?"

Father Gonzales pulled a leather-bound book from his front coat pocket and turned to a bookmark pressed between the pages. "I'd rather read it to you than attempt to summarize it—if you don't mind. But brace yourselves. I'm afraid it's quite scandalous and upsetting."

"Don't worry about us, Father," Sue said. "We can take it."

With a nod, Father Gonzales said, "This entry is dated September 2, 1908:

*A new nun has been sent to us from the Ursuline Convent in New Orleans to help with the teaching of the now almost one hundred students living at Holy Family Mission Boarding School. I requested three but will have to make do.*

*Sister Alma is seventeen years old, stands at five feet and two inches, and weighs less than 100 pounds. She is shy and modest—and respectably so—but seems unhappy to be here. An initial exam proved her to be proficient in high-level mathematics and the sciences—a rarity among the sisters—but she doesn't seem capable of maintaining order with the younger students. This afternoon, I told the Mother Superior that Sister Alma should be reassigned to the upper grades.*

*At that time, the Mother Superior informed me that Sister Alma had a reputation for falling in love. Mother Drexel fears that the sister took orders only by the command of her father. The Mother Superior at the Ursuline Convent in New Orleans may have sent her to us to get rid of her.*

Father Gonzales cleared his throat. "Father Galdas goes on to write about other matters concerning the food shortage, the horrendous winds, the problems with runaway students, the conflicts with angry parents, and so forth, and then, in an entry written the very next day, he writes:

*Today I witnessed Sister Alma lunching with the senior students. I'm alarmed by the way she spoke with one of our senior boys. I found it highly inappropriate. I asked her to come see me and the Mother Superior in my office this afternoon, where I warned her not to be overly friendly with the pupils, especially the boys. Although Sister Alma was polite, she hardly defended herself or made excuses, and I'm not reassured or convinced that her behavior won't continue.*

"Excuse me, Father," Sue said. "Is there any way that you could fast-forward to the scandalous and upsetting parts?"

"Sue," Tanya chastised beneath her breath.

"I'm nearly there," the priest said. "Let me see. Okay, here it is. This is dated December 20th, 1908:

*Today I was visited by Mr. Vincent Marcello, the father of Sister Alma. He traveled here from New Orleans, red-faced and angry, to accuse me of neglect. He claimed that his daughter had been abused by an older student and was now with-child. Mr. Marcello blamed me for this crime, for not running a tighter ship, as he called it. He demanded that his daughter should keep her holy orders and, after a discreet birth, be returned to Ursuline Convent. Mr. Marcello also insisted that the perpetrator be arrested and imprisoned or put to death.*

*When I questioned Sister Alma on the subject, she broke into tears and said she couldn't talk about it. However, in the end, I did get the name of her abuser: Randal Smith, a twelfth grader who has been with us since the turn of the century.*

"Rabbit raped Sister Alma?" Sue asked.

"That's what Mr. Marcello claimed," Father Gonzales said. "And I believed it, too, until this fell out of the book."

The Jesuit priest lifted a folded piece of parchment from the book and opened it.

"This is a letter written to Father Galdas by Sister Alma on February 2, 1909:

*Dear Father Galdas,*

*I wish I had the courage to speak up when my father came and yelled at you. I hope you will find it in your heart to forgive me. My father refuses to listen, but maybe you will. Randal Smith did not rape me. We fell in love.*

*I know you think, like the others, that Randal has run away from the law, but I know the truth. My father killed him. I haven't stopped weeping since.*

*Please don't send me back to Ursuline Convent. I will work hard if you allow me and my baby to stay. If you carry out my father's demands and separate us, I will have no choice but to follow my poor, sweet Rabbit into the river of death.*

*Yours Truly,*

*Alma Marcello*

Ellen recalled her dream with the white buffalo. "What do you think this means? Did Alma's father kill Rabbit?"

The Jesuit priest rubbed his chin. "I can think of no reason why Sister Alma would make up this story, can you? It seems to me that it must be true."

"I agree," Sue said.

"Do you know what happened to her and the baby?" Tanya asked.

"She delivered the child—a boy—at Holy Family Mission on June 20, 1909," the priest said. "Not long after, the baby was taken by another Ursuline nun to the convent in New Orleans."

"What about Sister Alma?" Ellen asked.

"Father Galdas writes in an entry dated June 25, 1909 that Alma went missing. They conducted a search but found no sign of her. He speculates that the poor girl either ran away or killed herself."

"How sad," Tanya said. "Her father was such a bully. It makes me so angry."

"And we're no closer to finding Rabbit's body," Ellen said.

Sue cocked her head to the side. "What do you think Sister Alma meant when she said that she would have no choice but to follow Rabbit into the river of death?"

"I assumed it was a figure of speech," Father Gonzales said. "An allusion to the river of death in the Greek Underworld."

"Is there a river near where the school would have been?" Ellen asked.

"Yes," the priest said with his brows lifted.

Ellen laced her fingers together and hesitated before asking, "Father, how do you feel about paranormal investigations?"

The Jesuit priest frowned. "I'm afraid I'm somewhat of a skeptic. I believe in an afterlife, of course, but most of what I've seen on television looks gimmicky."

"Ellen knows just how you feel," Sue said. "Isn't that right, Ellen?"

"Yes, I do. And it's not my intention to persuade you."

"I'd love for you to try," he said with a smile.

Ellen and her friends told him about the investigation at Talks to Buffalo Lodge, about the crows, and about Ellen's dream.

"Rabbit said he was murdered?" the priest asked with his eyes and mouth wide in surprise.

"It could be a coincidence," Ellen admitted.

"But a strange one, indeed," the priest conceded. "What do you plan to do next?"

"I'd like to convince the authorities to search the river," Ellen said.

Father Gonzales rubbed his chin. "I doubt you could make a case for it. The river runs for over thirty miles from Holy Family to the east past Rock City before joining the Marias River. Even if Alma and Randal *did* die in the Two-Medicine River near the school, their bodies could be miles away."

Sue lifted a finger. "Then we'll get one of those tour boats to take us for a special trip, late at night, when the spirits tend to make themselves known."

"Great idea!" Ellen said.

Tanya crossed her arms. "I don't know."

"Don't you want to help Crow Woman find peace after all these years?" Ellen asked her friend.

"Not really," Tanya said. "Not after she tried to kill us."

"What about Rabbit?" Sue asked. "Sister Alma may be able to help us to find his body. Wouldn't it be nice if he could be at rest?"

"Yes," Tanya said. "I suppose it would."

"Then we're doing this?" Ellen asked her friends.

"Please tell me I can come, too," the priest said with a smile.

CHAPTER NINE

# A Different Kind of Boat Tour

I t took every bit of Sue's powers of persuasion over the phone to convince the owner of a local tour company to allow her to charter a boat for a night cruise on the river. The owner didn't object to the tour taking place at night; it was the *river* that bothered him. He said again and again that he would prefer to provide a tour of any of the many beautiful lakes that the area afforded, for however long she wished, but he couldn't have known that his efforts were futile.

In the end, he yielded, and, two days later, he met Ellen, Sue, Tanya, and Father Gonzales just before sunset at a boat dock about five miles southeast of Browning.

The *Sinopah* was a long white wooden barge with light blue trim. With enough bench seating for twenty people, it looked more like a trolley than a boat because of its flat roof and six windows along each side. As soon as Ellen stepped onto it from the dock, with the help of the priest, she could tell, by the way the boards groaned beneath her, that it was a very old vessel.

The owner of the barge was Captain Scott, a man in his early fifties with brown eyes and long blond and gray hair and a short beard to match. His skin was tan and wrinkled from overexposure to the sun. Even beneath his fur-lined jacket, Ellen could tell he had wide shoulders and muscular arms, which made her feel like she and her friends were in good hands.

Ellen found herself coveting the captain's thick jacket and Father Gonzales's puffer coat and kid gloves. She and her friends, having lived through decades of the Texas summer heat, couldn't have known how terribly cold the wind blew on the rivers of Montana after dusk in July. Ellen shivered in her cable-knit cardigan, pulling it more tightly around her.

Because her ankle was still tender, she immediately found a seat on one of the middle benches. Tanya slid in beside her.

"Welcome aboard," the captain said as Sue and Father Gonzales made their way to a bench across the aisle from Tanya. "Are there any particular views you want to see before nightfall?"

"Not really," Sue said. "We aren't here for the views."

"Oh? Then why *are* we here?" Captain Scott asked.

"Um," Ellen glanced over at Father Gonzales, who waited patiently for Ellen and her friends to explain. "We're here to conduct a paranormal investigation."

The captain's bushy blond brows shot up. "Hmm. This is a first."

Father Gonzales smiled. "This is a first for me, too. It ought to prove interesting."

"So long as I get paid and you don't break any laws, I don't care what you do," the captain said.

The sun dropped behind the distant mountains beyond the grassy plains, and the wind picked up and formed waves with white caps running across the surface of the river. Although the passengers were protected from the wind in the shelter of the boat with the windows closed, the chill managed to find its way inside. Ellen covered her mouth, exhaled hot air onto her hands, and then covered her ears to warm them, but her efforts did little to alleviate the cold as the captain set off.

"What do we do now?" the priest asked.

Sue pulled a cannister of salt from her bag. "We create a circle of protection."

Since the boat rocked with the choppy water, Tanya, who had the best balance of the three friends, offered to pour the salt while Ellen and Sue lit the candles.

When Tanya approached the captain, where he stood at the helm, he said, "Not here, please."

"It's for your protection," Tanya argued.

"I'd rather not have salt on my dash. Keep it on the floor, where I can sweep it out."

"Then I can't include you in the circle," Tanya pointed out.

"I'm sure I'll be fine."

Tanya frowned but did as he said.

Sue put a handful of snacks on the bench between her and Father Gonzales.

"They attract the spirits," she explained.

Father Gonzales seemed unable to hide his smile of skepticism. "Whatever you say."

"I think you'll have to hold the candles," Tanya said when Sue attempted to place one on the floor near the circle of salt. "What if they fall over and catch the boat on fire?

"Good point," Sue said. "Which way is north?"

"That way." The captain pointed in Sue's direction.

"Perfect," Sue said. "I'll hold the northern, and Tanya, you can hold the southern."

Ellen took out her copper dousing rods. "I think we should start with these."

"That makes sense," Tanya agreed, returning to her seat.

"Are we anywhere near Holy Family Mission?" Sue asked the captain.

"I don't rightly know. This isn't my usual route."

Father Gonzales gazed through the windows on the other side of Sue. "I believe we're still a few miles away."

"Well, there's no harm in getting started, I suppose," Ellen said. Then she took a deep breath, held the rods in each hand, parallel to one another, and said, "Oh, spirits of the other realm, or of this realm too, we come in peace. We're here to help. If anyone is there, please look for the light of our candles. Smell the aroma of our snacks. Use the energy from the elements or from our cell phones to cross these rods, as a sign of your willingness to communicate with us."

She stared at the rods, which trembled because she was trembling and because the boat was rocking. She began to doubt that the rods would work under such conditions. It was too hard to hold them still.

"I wonder if the pendulum might work better," Sue suggested.

Ellen stuffed the rods back into her bag and pulled out the pendulum. Although it was impossible to hold the pendant still, there was the possibility that a spirit could manipulate the movement to communicate with them.

Ellen repeated her plea to the spirits, asking that they move the pendulum right to left if they were willing to speak with her.

The pendulum moved in a circle. Ellen held out her arm, hoping the movement would shift, but it remained consistent. The spirits weren't answering.

After a while, Father Gonzalez said, "Perhaps the captain should slow down. We're nearing the southern boundary of Holy Family Mission."

The captain glanced at Sue, who nodded. He slowed the boat from what had felt like thirty miles an hour to half that speed. At the slower speed, the rocking of the boat became more dramatic, and Ellen found herself having to hold on to the side of the bench to avoid bumping into Tanya.

"The old dormitories use to be near that bank, just to the north of us," Father Gonzales said.

"Could you take the boat a little closer to the bank?" Sue asked the captain.

"Aye, aye, matey," Captain Scott said.

Ellen reached out to the spirits again, this time calling Alma Marcello by name. Again, the pendulum did not change direction. It continued to swing in a circular motion.

"Don't get discouraged," Sue said. "Do you want me to take over?"

"No, that's okay."

The sun made its complete descent, and the only light to see by came from an electric lantern hanging on a hook above the captain's head and their two candles. The river itself became dark with only a sliver of a moon in a cloudy, starless sky. Lights on the exterior of the boat helped them to see a few yards in each direction. The horizon had all but disappeared.

Ellen repeated her appeal to Alma Marcello. She was beginning to believe the trip had been a waste of time and money when, to her surprise, the pendulum swung sharply to the right and left.

"Wait. I might have flinched or something," Ellen said, wanting to be sure. "Let's try that again." She steadied the pendant and said, "Alma Marcello, the Ursuline nun from New Orleans, if you're there, please know we come in peace. We only want to help you. If you're there and willing to speak with us, please make the pendulum swing to my right and left."

The pendulum swung with such force that Ellen had to tighten her grip on the string.

She looked up at her friends with excitement.

"How can you be sure that Alma is causing that to happen and not a nasty demon?" Father Gonzales asked.

"Usually we ask questions that only the spirit we're trying to contact would know the answers to," Sue explained.

"And how does the spirit answer such questions?" the priest asked.

Sue pulled the Ouija Board and planchette from her bag. "With this."

Father Gonzales shook his head. "No, no, no. Not that. Everyone knows that you're only inviting demon possession by using such a thing."

"We're protected by our circle," Ellen explained.

Tanya glanced back at the captain. "At least, most of us are."

"You should have told me about this before I agreed to come," the priest said.

"You should have asked more questions about our methods," Sue argued. "You're the one who wanted to come. We didn't twist your arm."

Ellen gave him a sympathetic look. "I understand your concerns, but it's the only way we know how to get specific answers."

The priest shrugged and lifted his hands in resignation. "This is your show. I'm just along for the ride."

"Good," Sue said. "Would you hold this please?" She handed him the candle, and he took it.

Ellen turned to the captain, "Could you stop here?"

"Do you want me to anchor her down?" the captain asked. "I don't recommend it."

"I don't think so," Ellen said.

The captain did as she asked, allowing the boat to idle and drift in the rough water along the northern shore. Then Sue traded places with Tanya and put the board on the bench beside Ellen. Turning toward one another in their seats, Sue and Ellen gently placed their fingertips on the planchette.

"Alma Marcello," Sue said. "Please use this board to communicate with us." Sue moved the planchette across the board as she explained about the letters, numbers, and the yes and no positions. "To start, please tell us the year of your birth."

Ellen's fingers nearly slipped from the plastic indicator as it quickly moved to 1-8-9-1.

"Are you doing that?" Father Gonzales asked Sue.

"No," she said. "I'd swear on a Bible, if you had one."

The priest looked suspiciously at Ellen.

"I'd swear on one, too," she said.

The captain scoffed. "Yeah. Right."

"Ask another question," the priest urged them.

"Thank you, Alma," Sue said. "To make sure we have the right Alma, could you tell us the name of your baby's father?"

The electric lantern over the captain's head flickered as the plastic indicator spelled R-A-B-B-I-T.

The priest shook his head. "Maybe you aren't aware that you're moving it."

Ellen shrugged. "Maybe."

"Thank you, Alma," Sue said. "Rabbit is missing. Do you know where his body is?"

The planchette flew across the board to YES.

The electric lantern flickered again before going out.

"Hells bells," the captain muttered. "Just what we need with the wind picking up."

He took the lantern from its hook and gave it a whack, but the light did not come back on. He reached into a compartment near the helm and took out a flashlight.

Sue said, "Thank you, Alma. That's good news. Is Rabbit's body in this river?"

The boat rocked sharply to the right, causing everyone to sway to one side in their seats. Once they regained their balance, Ellen and Sue returned their fingertips to the planchette indicator.

Sue said, "Alma Marcello, is Rabbit in this river?"

The planchette circled around the board and returned to YES.

Sue and Ellen beamed at one another.

"Will you lead us to him, Alma?" Ellen asked.

The planchette circled around the board and returned to YES.

"How will she do that?" Father Gonzales asked.

"We'll try the dousing rods again," Ellen said.

The boat rocked hard to one side again. Ellen held onto her seat until the boat steadied and she could reach into her bag for the rods. Then, as before, she held them in front of her, parallel to one another. With the rocking of the boat, they swung side to side, but she hoped they might still prove useful.

"Alma Marcello," she began. "As we move closer to the location of Rabbit's body, please bring the rod tips together. As we move further away from it, please move the rod tips apart."

The boat engine quit idling. Ellen glanced over at the captain, who shifted the gear and turned the key. The engine turned but wouldn't start. He tried again, twisting the key this way and that. He changed the gear, twisted the key. Then he pounded his fist on the dash.

"The battery must be dead," the captain said angrily. "I swear it's a new battery. It must have been bad to begin with."

Ellen glanced nervously at her friends just as the dousing rods yanked on her arms. They didn't cross together or push apart; instead, they pulled her toward the side of the boat, toward the northern shore.

With her eyes wide and full of excitement, Ellen climbed to her feet. Sue moved into the aisle and out of the way as Ellen limped toward the door leading to the outer deck. Father Gonzales jumped up, handed off his candle, and followed her. When he opened the door, the wind howled against them. The pull on the roads was so strong that Ellen nearly lost her balance.

The priest helped her to the side of the boat, where the dousing rods tugged her upper body over the rail, toward the river. Ellen's stomach pressed hard against the rail as her arms stretched down toward the raging river.

"Help!" Ellen cried. "They're pulling me in!"

Father Gonzales grabbed her waist with both hands and held onto her as he shouted, "Stop the boat!"

"There's no way to stop her," the captain shouted. "And we'll be ripped to shreds if I lower the anchor now!"

The boat dipped sharply forward, plunging Ellen's arms underwater.

"Let go of the rods!" the priest shouted against the wind.

"But this may be our only way to find Rabbit!" she shouted back.

Just then, the other side of the boat lifted high in the air and tossed Ellen and the priest overboard.

Ellen clung to the dousing rods as she fell through the dark, freezing water. She'd been afraid to let go, lest she lose her only chance of finding Rabbit; but now, feeling frozen to her core and desperately out of breath, she let them go and kicked and flailed toward the surface. Her tender ankle throbbed with pain. For a moment she felt transported, as if she had become trapped inside Weeping Wall.

When she finally reached air, she sucked in water by mistake and coughed as she struggled to stay above the waves. The boat could barely be seen in the distance. Without a battery, it wouldn't be coming for her anytime soon.

She looked around for Father Gonzales.

"Over here!" he cried.

Beneath the dim light of the sliver of a moon, she saw him standing in waist-deep water about twenty yards away, waving his arms over his head. But he was west of her, and the river was carrying her in the opposite direction. She struggled against the current toward the grassy bank in the distance until her feet could finally reach the river floor. Then, trying her best not to overextend her sprained ankle, she limped toward land as the cold wind hurled her cardigan like a loose, flapping sail, behind her.

# CHAPTER TEN

# The Lady of the River

L ater that night, Ellen sat wrapped in blankets before a warm fire in the rectory at Holy Family Mission. She sat in a wingback chair across from Father Gonzales, who had changed into clean at-tire—a sweater and trousers—and was washing and drying her clothes in the laundry room down the hall. They each sipped hot cups of coffee to warm their bones while they waited to hear back from the authorities about the *Sinopah* and its passengers.

Ellen was worried sick. What if the boat had capsized and her friends had drowned?

"Are you sure you're okay?" Father Gonzales asked her again. "Can't I get you anything else? Perhaps something to eat?"

"I'm fine," she said. "I'm just so thankful that one of your parishion-ers happened to be driving by. I don't think I could have walked much further."

"Me, too." He took a sip of his coffee. "Speaking of parishion-ers...something has just occurred to me."

"Oh? What is it?"

"Father O'Brien and I have often exchanged stories about people who claim to have seen a lady on the river."

"A lady? What do they say about her?"

"Interestingly, and perhaps not coincidentally, they describe her as a young nun standing on the surface of the river."

Ellen raised her brows. "Really? Oh, my gosh! Do you think they're describing Sister Alma?"

"That's what I'm wondering."

"Has anyone reported anything else about her? Has she spoken to them?"

He rubbed his chin. "They say she beckons them but doesn't speak. They seem to have seen her at the same place—where the river turns south. That's what's been most convincing to Father O'Brien and me. People describe the exact same spot."

"Is it anywhere close to the spot where we fell in?"

"It's further east, actually."

"Oh." Ellen was disappointed. If people *had* seen the lady at the exact spot where the rods pulled her under, then she would feel certain that Rabbit's remains could be found there. "How many people have claimed to have seen her?"

"Oh, dozens over the years. Father O'Brien and I were hoping it was the blessed mother."

"I suppose it could be."

"Yes, but I wonder…"

"Yes?"

"Do you suppose it's possible that the body of Rabbit might be lying below the river where those dousing rods pulled you and I overboard and that the body of Sister Alma might be found further east where people have claimed to have seen the lady?"

The corners of Ellen's mouth stretched into a wide grin. "Yes, Father. I *do* think that's possible."


Ellen was awakened by the ringing of a telephone. She opened her eyes to find that she'd fallen asleep in the wingback chair of the rectory, still bundled in blankets near the fire. Across from her, Father Gonzales, who had also fallen asleep, was opening his eyes and crossing the room to the landline phone.

"Hello?" he said into the phone. A moment later, he said, "That's great news. Thank you, Officer."

He hung up the phone and turned to Ellen with a smile. "They found the boat. Its passengers are safe. Your friends are on their way to your hotel now. Are you ready for me to drive you back?"

"If my clothes are dry," she said, as relief swept through her. "I would imagine they are by now."

The priest's face turned bright red. "Oh, I'd forgotten. Of course. Please, follow me, and I'll show you where you can dress."


Sue and Tanya were waiting for Ellen in the lobby of Glacier Park Lodge. As soon as Father Gonzales helped her through the lobby door, she was accosted by their eager embraces.

"Thank God!" Tanya cried.

"We were so worried!" Sue said. "We were sure you were dead."

"Well, as you can see, we're alive and well," Ellen said with a laugh. "I'm relieved to see *you* safe and sound, too. What a night!"

"What an adventure," Father Gonzales said. "I suppose the next step would be to hire divers to search for the bodies."

"Yes," Sue agreed. "You wouldn't happen to know anyone, would you, Father?"

"Now that I think of it, I do know a parishioner who's a certified diver. I'll give him a call in the morning."

"Oh, thank you," Ellen said, squeezing the priest's hands. "Thank you for everything."

"And please keep us posted on the search," Tanya asked.

"Can you make it to your room from here?" Father Gonzales asked Ellen.

"Yes, thanks again. You go home and try to get some sleep. We'll do the same."

The Jesuit priest left with a wave, and Ellen was helped by Sue and Tanya to the lobby elevators.

"What a night," Tanya said, echoing Ellen.

"Oh, here's your purse," Sue said, handing the shoulder bag over to Ellen. "Your phone has been ringing like crazy."

"What?"

The elevator doors opened. A girl of perhaps twenty stepped out before Ellen and her friends stepped in.

Ellen looked at her phone. "It's Brian. He's called six times. I hope nothing's wrong."

She listened to one of his messages and was relieved. From the slur of his speech, it was clear he'd been drinking. He poured out his heart and soul. He missed her and wanted to be with her.

They reached their floor as Ellen said, "He's fine. Just drunk."

Before they could ask about it, she added, "So, tell me what happened, after Father Gonzales and I fell overboard."

"Well, this may be hard to believe," Sue said as she and Tanya helped Ellen to her room. "But we think Sister Alma may have saved our lives."

Ellen stopped in her tracks. "Really? What makes you think that?"

"The man who found us said the lady of the river led him to us," Tanya said.

Sue put her hands on her hips. "And when we asked him what she looked like, he said she was a young nun with a beautiful face, and she walked on water."

Ellen grinned. "He's not the first to have seen her."

As her friends helped her into her room, Ellen told them what Father Gonzales had said about the lady of the river.

Ellen spent the next day resting in her room. She slept through breakfast, ordered room service for lunch, and then took a nap. Sue and Tanya offered to bring supper to her room and had just arrived when Father Gonzales called.

"I saw her!" he said gleefully over the phone. "I saw the lady of the river!"

"Really?" Ellen said as she glanced across the room at her friends. "What happened? Did you find any remains?"

"We did! My friend the diver found the remains of *two* bodies—one where we went overboard and the other where the lady appeared—where she always appears."

Tears welled in Ellen's eyes. "Thank heavens!"

"That's if the bodies are indeed the remains of Rabbit and Sister Alma. The police are pulling them up from the river now. I've been told it may take a few days to identify them."

"Oh, I can hardly wait!"

"By the way, the diver found your dousing rods, too. I'll give them to you the next time I see you. Father O'Brien gave me quite a look when he saw me with them."

Ellen laughed. "I bet he did."

"Isn't this exciting?"

"It certainly is!" Ellen said. "I hope we've found Rabbit and Sister Alma. I pray it's them!"

"You and me both!"

"Did you ever hear back from the Ursuline Convent about the baby sent there in 1909?" Ellen asked. She'd been thinking about something the white buffalo had said to her in her dream—about the hide belonging to someone else. If there were a baby, the hide would belong to it.

"Not yet. Wouldn't that be the icing on the cake? If the convent has adoption records and we found the descendant of Rabbit and Alma?"

"Yes, it would. Please keep us posted on both fronts."

"Will do!"

Ellen hung up the phone and was in the process of telling her friends the priest's good news when Sue's phone rang.

"Hold on a minute," Sue said to Ellen. "It's Karen Murray."

With her ear to her phone, Sue said, "Hello, Karen…This Saturday? Why, yes. We would be happy to come. Thank you for inviting us."

Sue hung up the phone and returned it to her purse.

"Well?" Tanya asked.

"We've just been invited to participate in the Blackfeet's annual Sun Dance this weekend."

# CHAPTER ELEVEN

# The Sun Dance

When Ellen and her friends arrived via taxi to the Badger-Two Medicine on Saturday morning, they were surprised by all the vehicles parked along the road. There were at least fifty and possibly more. Careful not to hurt her ankle, Ellen followed her friends through the tall pines and to the top of the open valley, where they were even more shocked to find the wilderness below littered with dozens of teepees, sweat lodges, and a large center structure from which the sound of drums carried.

"It looks like they've been here for a while," Sue said.

There were campfires, ice chests, and people in lawn chairs, and there were young children running around playing a game with rocks. A few women sat on blankets visiting as they watched the children. Three men were wrapping a twenty-foot-tall teepee frame with painted canvas.

Weaving through the grounds was a line of dancers in feathered headdresses, moccasins, and beaded gowns. The dancers were arranged from the tallest to the shortest, including old and young alike. They bent their knees and bounced to the beat of the drums.

Spectators sang, clapped, and waved as this parade made its way into the center structure where most of the spectators followed.

Ellen and her friends trekked down the steep slope toward the festivities. Not finding anyone they recognized, the ladies followed the others into the big center structure, where the sound of the singing and drumming grew louder.

Inside the large dome, Ellen and her friends found the dancers and spectators numbered over sixty people. Most stood in a few rows around the perimeter of the room bending their knees and stamping their feet to the beat of the drums as they hummed and whistled along. Another row sat on the ground in front of the ring of dancers. A thick central pole, forked at the top and colorfully decorated, was surrounded at the bottom by four drummers and a few more dancers.

Ellen soon spotted people she recognized—Jack Stone on the outer perimeter, Rich Falcon at the drums, and Eric Old Person sitting in a position of prominence. Along the opposite side, she noticed Karen Murray sitting with a group of women. With tears in her eyes, Karen watched the three dancers in the center of the room, a few yards from the drummers.

That's when Ellen had the greatest shock of all. The three male dancers nearest the drummers were bleeding on their chests where sticks had been inserted beneath the skin at the top of their breasts and tied to ropes that were tethered to the top of the central post. The three men wore wreaths of dried sage and held a bunch of it between their lips. As they danced to the beat of the drums, they leaned away from the post to which they were tethered, essentially ripping the skin from their chests a little at a time.

"Oh my God," Tanya whispered. "Is that Terry Murray?"

"I think it is," Sue said.

Terry danced between two others. All three men had tears streaming from their eyes as they endured their self-inflicted pain. Ellen glanced back at Karen who was watching her husband's torment with tear-stained cheeks.

Ellen and her friends observed the dancing with fascination for another half hour when they noticed a few of the people, including Jack Stone, had begun to exit the dome.

"Let's go talk to Jack," Ellen whispered to Sue and Tanya.

"Good idea," Sue said.

Ellen followed Sue and Tanya toward the exit. As Ellen was about to leave the dome, she glanced back once more at Terry Murray and was surprised to find him looking back at her. She shuddered and stepped out into the sunny morning light.

Sue and Tanya had already caught up with Jack Stone, who was standing beside a petite woman and holding a sleepy little girl, about six years old. He was saying, "Yes, we've been at it in the medicine lodge since sunset."

"Don't you mean *sunrise?*" Sue asked.

"Sunset," Jack said again. "We came a few days ago to prepare and set up, but the dancing started last night at sunset."

"I bet you're tired," Ellen said.

Jack turned to the petite woman beside him. "Marjorie, these are the ladies from Texas I was telling you about."

"Hello," Marjorie said. "I'm Jack's wife. It's nice to meet you."

Although she appeared to be in her early sixties, the lines in her face were deep, perhaps from smoking or from overexposure to the sun.

"It's nice to meet you," Ellen said.

A younger woman as petite as Marjorie walked up and said, "There you are."

She held out her arms to the sleepy little girl.

Jack passed the girl to the young woman and said, "And this is my daughter, Jan, and my granddaughter, Joy."

"How nice to meet you," Sue said. "Jan was my mother's name."

"What a pretty little girl," Tanya added.

"Thank you," Jan said.

"My family and I are going back to our lodge for some breakfast," Jack said to Ellen and her friends. "Would you care to join us?"

"Thank you, but we've already eaten," Ellen said.

Sue lifted a hand in the air. "But we'd love to join you anyway. Thanks so much for the invitation."

Tanya gave Ellen a look that said, *get us out of this*, but Ellen wanted to go with Jack, because she wanted to find out why Terry Murray was hurting himself.

They followed Jack and his family to a large teepee, where an older woman was already sitting, cross-legged on a blanket.

"Niksista, Anistawa Naapiianamayia'ki Sue Graham, Ellen Mohr, and Tanya, er…"

"Sanchez," Tanya said.

"This is my mother," Jack said. "Sinopa."

"That was the name of our boat," Ellen said. "What does it mean?"

"Fox," Jack said.

"Nitsikinonootsi," the older woman said.

"Please sit down." Jack pointed to a blanket on the ground. "I'll bring in the food."

Ellen and her friends sat together on one side of the teepee. Across from them, Marjorie sat beside Sinopa, and Jan sat beside her mother with her daughter in her lap. Joy's eyes were now closed, and she appeared to be asleep.

"Was she up all night?" Ellen asked of the little girl.

"Most of it," Jan replied. "Are you enjoying your trip?"

Although Ellen didn't think *enjoy* was quite the right word, considering she'd almost died twice, she said, "Oh, yes."

Jack returned with eight foil packets and gave one to each person. "Be careful. They're hot."

Ellen wasn't hungry, but not wishing to be rude, she accepted the warm packet, which she, like the others, set on the blanket near her crossed legs. Opening it up, she found a big, toasted bun with egg and bacon inside."

"This looks delicious," Sue said. "Thank you."

Marjorie then passed them each a juice box.

"Thank you," Tanya said.

Jack settled in on the other side of his mother. "Karen said she was going to invite you. Are you enjoying the Sun Dance so far?"

"It's very interesting," Sue said.

Jack and Marjorie laughed.

"You're wondering about the blood ritual," Jan said. "White people are always quick to judge us, aren't they, Dad?"

"I meant no offense," Sue said before taking a bite of her breakfast sandwich.

"But we are curious as to why Terry, or anyone, would want to put himself through that," Ellen added.

Jack nodded. "I understand. Well, you'll recall from our purification ceremony that Terry has a drinking problem."

Ellen and her friends nodded.

"He's been dry for over a week. In participating in this ritual, he makes an oath before the entire community, and he makes this sacrifice to Creator on behalf of the community. He and the other two men pay homage to Sun and Mother Earth and ask Sun to help them to be brave and strong and worthy of a new life."

"That's what the Sun Dance is for," Marjorie added. "It's about renewal. We do it at this time every year to invoke the sun and the earth to continue to rejuvenate the land's resources and the creativity of the people who live on it."

Just then, Ellen's cell phone rang. Worried that she'd offended them, she quickly fished the phone from her purse and silenced the ringer. But, seeing that the call was from Father Gonzales, she said, "Please excuse me. I have to take this call."

She climbed from the teepee and out into the bright day, where others were dancing or visiting. One older man dragged the skulls of two large beasts—perhaps steers or buffalos—behind him as he danced among the others.

"Hello, Father?" Ellen said into the phone.

"Ellen! I'm glad I caught you. I have news—good and not so good."

"Tell me!"

"Could you and your friends come to the rectory? I'd love to discuss it in person."

"I'm afraid we're at the Blackfeet Sun Dance for most of the day. Can't you tell me over the phone? I'm dying to know."

A few minutes later, Ellen returned to the teepee where Jack Stone, his family, and Ellen's friends were finishing up their breakfast. Ellen sat beside Tanya and said, "That was Father Gonzales. He had news about the remains."

"I was just telling Jack and his family the story of Rabbit and Sister Alma," Sue said. "What's the news? Were the authorities able to identify the bodies?"

"They were able to identify Sister Alma," Ellen said. "They found a rosary wrapped around one of her hands, and her name was engraved on the back of the cross, along with the year 1907. It's not conclusive evidence, but, together with the letters of Father Galdas, it seems to be enough."

"That's fantastic!" Sue cried.

"But what about Rabbit?" Tanya asked.

"Unfortunately, the authorities are having a harder time with the second body," Ellen said. "Apparently, there aren't any dental or medical records. Father Gonzales is reading through every journal, letter, and document he can find, hoping to discover the mention of a characteristic that might prove the body is Rabbit."

"Why not ask his mother, Maisto Aakii?" Jack's mother said.

"Maisto Aakii means Crow Woman," Jack explained.

Ellen and her friends told them what had happened the last time they'd visited Talks to Buffalo Lodge.

"The spirits are open during the time of the Sun Dance," Sinopa said. "Take a medicine man or woman with you, do the Sun Dance, and Maisto Aakii will want to answer."

Ellen glanced at her friends and back at Jack. "Where do we find a medicine man or woman?"

"My mother is a medicine woman," Jack said, "but she needs to stay here to pray for Joy's healing."

"Karen is a medicine woman," Sinopa said.

"But doesn't she need to stay to pray for her husband?" Sue asked.

"She needs to get away from here," Sinopa said. "Terry must fight his own battle."

Once they'd finished their breakfast, Jack climbed to his feet. "Come on. I'll take you to Karen, and we can see if she's willing to help you."

It was almost noon when Ellen and her friends arrived with Karen Murray in her black Honda Accord at Talks to Buffalo Lodge. At first, Tanya insisted that she would wait in the car, but when Ellen reminded her of the rock that nearly hit her in the head while she was sitting in the rental, Tanya came to the conclusion that no place was safe, so she may as well go inside.

"We have a medicine woman with us this time," Sue reminded her as they made their way to the front door. "And we'll make our circle of protection. It kept me safe last time."

They carried pipes made of the bones of eagles. The pipes had soft eagle feathers fastened to them with string. Karen had a buckskin drum, and Ellen brought the duffle bag containing some of their smaller equipment, including the Ouija Board.

Although she was determined to speak with Crow Woman, Ellen was also frightened. She hoped Sinopa had been right in saying that Crow Woman would be open because of the Sun Dance.

Just to be safe, they made their circle of protection with salt and four candles. They put some snacks and water bottles in the center of it.

"We usually do this at night," Sue said. "That's when the ghosts tend to be more active."

Karen moved to the center of their circle. "Why don't you stand there with the pipes, and I'll show you the dance? It's very simple."

Ellen and her friends moved to one side as Karen pounded a quick, even beat on her drum.

"Bend your knees like this," Karen said. "And then blow through the pipes with the beat. The sound of the pipes is meant to emulate the call of the eagle, a sacred bird to Sun."

Ellen and her friends did as Karen said.

"Now we face the east," Karen said, turning toward the kitchen. A few beats later, she said, "And now we face the west." They turned toward the master bedroom.

After a few more minutes of dancing, Karen set down her drum. Ellen and her friends stopped blowing through the pipes.

Karen lifted her palms and said something in her native tongue.

All four candles went out. The fluorescent tube in the kitchen flickered. An old book that had been lying on the floor lifted into the air and struck the wall. Ellen wondered if it was the same book that had smacked her in the head the last time she was here.

"I think we got her attention," Sue whispered.

Ellen took the Ouija Board and planchette from her duffle bag. She and Sue sat on the two metal chairs with the board balanced on their knees. Tanya and Karen knelt between them and placed their fingertips beside theirs on the plastic indicator.

Sue said, "Karen, could you ask Crow Woman if she's there?"

"Aoki tsakinohkanista' paispa, Maisto Aakii?" Karen said.

The planchette spelled N-A-T-S-I-I-K-S-N-I-I-K-I-S-K-A-A-A-T-S-I-S-T-A."

When the indicator stopped moving, Tanya whispered, "Does that mean something, Karen?"

"She's asking where her son is," Karen said.

Ellen frowned. "Can you tell her that we think we found him in Two-Medicine River? Tell her that we need her help identifying the body. Ask her if he ever broke a bone."

No sooner had Karen translated than the planchette flew across the board and spelled S-I-N-A-A-K-S-S-I-N-I.

The planchette paused.

"Book," Karen said. "But what does she mean?" She asked a question in her native tongue.

The old book flew up and struck a wall on the opposite side of the room.

"Does she want us to look at that book?" Sue asked.

"Where did it come from, anyway?" Ellen wondered.

Karen climbed to her feet and left the circle of protection to fetch the old book. "I've been in this house dozens of times and have never seen it."

"It came out of the floor the last time we were here," Sue said. "From over there, from in front of the hearth. You see where that floorboard has come loose?"

The old wooden floor in front of the fireplace was torn up. Had the book been hiding there?

Karen flipped through the yellowed pages as she returned to the circle. "It appears to be the memoir of Maisto Aakii."

Sue arched a brow. "It was written by Crow Woman? I didn't think Indian women could read or write back then."

"It's common for white women to underestimate the abilities of Indian women," Karen said.

Sue's face turned red. "I just meant it was so long ago. Most white women couldn't read or write back then, either."

"I think you're mistaken on both counts," Karen said. "Besides, this is dated 1935."

"That means she wrote it after the death of Talks to Buffalo," Ellen pointed out.

"It's a short memoir—more of a letter, really," Karen said. "Shall I read it?"

"Please do!" Sue said.

# CHAPTER TWELVE

# Crow Woman

Karen sat cross-legged on the floor beside Tanya. Sue and Ellen took their seats in the metal chairs. By the light of the candles, which Tanya had relit, and the little bit of sun coming in through the front windows, Karen read the memoir of Crow Woman aloud:

*My people called me Maisto Aakii (Crow Woman), because when I was a young girl of twelve summers, before I had begun to bleed, I was taken by a Crow to be his wife.*

*I did not like my Crow husband. His name was Tsikatsi (Grasshopper). He was handsome but unkind. His other wives were cruel to me. They called me lazy and unskilled, even though I worked harder than any of them. They stole the berries I picked and claimed them as their own. They stole the rabbits that I shot and the fish that I caught. If there was ever trouble, they blamed me. My Crow husband believed them and punished me. He whipped me with thorny branches.*

*I tried to run away three times. The third time, my husband punished me so severely, that I gave up the idea of ever returning to my people.*

*When Grasshopper died in a battle three summers after he took me, I asked the chief to let me return to my camp, since I had no children and since the other widows hated me. The chief said I could go if, and only if, I killed the fox that pestered and ate his turkeys.*

That night, I lay in wait at the bottom of a hill where the turkeys liked to roam. The favorite male with the longest snood was busy with one of the hens while the others slept in the tall grass.

I had a bow and quiver of arrows that Grasshopper had made for me when he first took me to his camp. They had served me well. I shot many rabbits with them. This night, I would shoot a fox.

The half-moon was bright, and I saw the fox as it crept toward the turkeys. I was fascinated by his stealth. I admired his skill. I also thought he was the cutest animal I had ever seen.

Something made me love the fox. I did not wish to bring him harm. I drew my arrow and pointed, but I did not aim for the fox. Instead, I shot one of the sleeping male turkeys and killed him.

The fox froze when my arrow struck. He looked up and spotted me as I slowly made my way toward the dead turkey. The other turkeys awoke and gobbled at me, distressed by my presence. All but one went away. One looked on as I pulled my arrow free of the dead turkey, picked it up by the legs, and threw it toward the fox.

The fox took my offering and ran away. I followed him and never looked back. When I came to the river, I followed it until I found the camp of my people. I slept in the grass until sunrise. When I awoke, the fox was lying a few feet away. I got up to look for my family, and the fox followed me until others came out of their lodges. Then the fox went away. I wanted to go after him, but I wanted to find my family more.

My people did not recognize me. They saw me dressed like the Crow and called me Maisto Aakii (Crow Woman). That is what I was called from that day on.

I was devastated to learn that my father and mother and brother were no longer among our people. No one knew where my family members were or if they were alive. I suspect my family went looking for me after my Crow husband abducted me. To this day, I do not know what became of them. If it had not been for my friend the fox, who returned to me that night, I would have flung myself into the river.

I built a lodge from willow saplings on the outskirts of the Gros Ventre camp. I wove thatches of long grass to cover it until I could get hides. The fox slept with me and kept me company. I caught fish and rabbits and shared my food with him. I called him Sinopa Iikanata'psiiwa (Cute Fox).

Not long after I had returned to the Gros Ventures, some men rode into the camp on horses. One was very tall and handsome. He had a white buffalo on the back of his horse.

I said, "Let me tan that hide for you."

"Who is this?" he asked some of the others.

"Crow Woman," they said. "She says she is Gros Venture, but no one knows her."

I said, "My father was Piegan (Blackfoot). He was called Aawakaasi (Antelope Hunter). My mother was Gros Venture. She was called Sohksiisiimstaan (Meadow Lark). My brother was called Miikaysi (Squirrel)."

"I am Piegan," the tall man said. "I knew your father. I am called Aisaistowa Iini (Talks to Buffalo)."

He invited me to join him and his friends at their lodge, where he watched me prepare the white buffalo hide while his friends cooked the meat. He spoke with me as I worked, and I told him about my life before and after I was taken by my Crow husband. When the meat was ready to eat, he gave me the tastiest part. That night, he took me as his wife.

At first, Cute Fox was too apprehensive to join me at the lodge of Talks to Buffalo and his friends. He stayed in my small lodge, where I took him food each day. Then one day, I lured him to the bigger lodge with pieces of meat. Talks to Buffalo was kind to Cute Fox, and they became friends.

After two new moons, Cute Fox and I went with Talks to Buffalo and his friends to his people, to my father's people, the Piegan. I was happy to talk to those who remembered my father. I wept with joy at the stories told by the Piegan of my father when he was a boy.

When I learned I was with-child, Talks to Buffalo, who had much wealth compared to other people, had a big lodge built in the style of the whites for us a few miles from the main village. Not long after, we had a son.

*First, we called him Iinaksipoka, or Baby. After two summers had come and gone, we called him A'atsita (Rabbit) because of how he walks. One leg is shorter than the other.*

*This was the happiest time of my life.*

"Wait a minute!" Ellen said, interrupting Karen's translation of Crow Woman's memoir. "That's the identifying characteristic we need to prove that the other body belongs to Rabbit! If one leg is shorter than the other, then it's him!"

Ellen suddenly recalled the dream she had in which the white buffalo had told her why he was named Rabbit. She'd forgotten until now.

"Call Father Gonzales!" Sue said.

Ellen plucked her phone from her purse and called the rectory.

"Hello?" Father Gonzales said over the phone.

"Father, it's Ellen."

"Oh, I'm so glad you called. I was just about to phone you with some exciting news."

"Really? What?" Ellen glanced at her friends as she put her phone on speaker.

"The Ursuline Convent has no records about a baby arriving in 1909 from here; however, Officer Jackson called a moment ago with a DNA match."

"What do you mean?" Sue said. "What kind of DNA match?"

"Oh, hello, Sue," the priest said.

"I have you on speaker, Father," Ellen explained. "I'm here with Sue, Tanya, and Karen Murray, a woman of the Blackfeet."

"Hello," Father Gonzales said.

Ellen paced the room within the circle of protection. "So, tell us about this DNA match."

"The authorities ran DNA from both remains through their various data bases and found someone in New Orleans, still alive today, who has a 75% match to *both* bodies."

"What does that mean?" Sue asked.

"That means that we've found a descendant of Sister Alma and the second body, which I'm determined to prove is Rabbit," the priest explained. "The descendant's name is Sidney Longfellow, and he lives in New Orleans."

"Did you say Sidney Longfellow?" Karen asked as she climbed to her feet.

"Yes," Father Gonzales said. "That's right."

Karen frowned. "That's the name of the CEO of Solonex, the oil and gas company that's suing the U.S. government for rights to drill on the Badger-Two Medicine."

Ellen's mouth fell open. "Can't there be more than one Sidney Longfellow?"

"In New Orleans?" Karen asked.

"It's a big city," Ellen pointed out.

"Father, how accurate are those DNA findings?" Sue asked.

"Very accurate, according to Officer Jackson."

Tanya stood up and brushed off her knees. "What do we do now?"

"Do you have any contact information for Mr. Longfellow?" Ellen asked.

"No phone number or email address. I've searched the Internet every which way I know how. I may have to leave it to the authorities to get ahold of him."

"We have exciting news, too, Father," Ellen said. "I'll explain later, but would you also ask the Medical Examiner to check if one leg is longer than the other on the second set of remains?"

"Of course. I'll get back with you soon."

"Thank you, Father," Ellen said. "Goodbye."

"Goodbye, ladies."

Ellen hung up the phone.

Then Tanya turned to Karen. "If Sidney Longfellow really is a Blackfoot descendant, maybe he'll change his mind about the Badger-Two Medicine."

"I doubt it will make a difference to the man," Karen said. "He only cares about one thing: money."

"Well, there's nothing more we can do until Father Gonzales hears back from the authorities," Ellen said. "Would you mind if we finish Crow Woman's memoir?"

"I don't mind," Karen said. She turned to Tanya and Sue. "Should I keep going?"

"That would be great," Tanya said.

Karen sat back down on the floor beside Tanya as Ellen took the metal chair across from Sue. Then Karen picked up from where she had left off:

*This was the happiest time of my life.*

*I strapped Rabbit to my back and rode out nearly every day with my husband to hunt or to fish or to shop for supplies in the village. Talks to Buffalo was full of Sun power. That is what our people said of him. He was full of the Sun power because he was good with hunting the buffalo. Some of our people paid him to shoot on their behalf.*

*Our wealth increased. I played a small part in it by tanning hides for others. I used the method I learned from the Crow. Only two good things came from my time with the Crow: Cute Fox and my skills in tanning hides.*

*We had many visitors come to our lodge. We fed them meat, along with vegetables we grew behind the house. After our meal, we sat with our guests before the warm hearth and engaged in storytelling, singing, or dancing. Sometimes a medicine man or woman came with a sacred pipe, and we smoked.*

*Rabbit had other children to play with every day. After we finished our daily jobs, he played with them at our house or at the lodges of our friends. We were always with our people. We were with them for the ceremonies and the rituals. We were also with them for visiting and good times.*

*After Rabbit's third summer, Cute Fox crossed the Rainbow Bridge. When we visited to the Two-Badger Medicine for prayer, I felt his spirit there. I thanked him for being my only friend at one of the lowest times of my life.*

*During Rabbit's fourth summer, the Holy Family Mission Boarding School came and took many of the children on the reservation away. The parents were angry. They spoke with the Indian Office, but nothing could be done. I became frightened that one day, the priests would take my Rabbit away from me. I told Talks to Buffalo that we should run away, but he said there was no place for us to go.*

*They came for Rabbit during his fifth summer. Talks to Buffalo and I refused to let him go. The Indian Office withheld the rations they supplied to our people from those who refused to give up their children. Many depended on the rations because the land on which we were allowed to hunt and farm had become smaller and smaller. Our people were no longer self-sufficient.*

*But my husband and I did not need the rations. Because we were self-sufficient, we managed to keep our son from being taken away until his ninth summer.*

*That summer, the men came to us with guns. They were not the priests but the officers from the Bureau. They threatened to imprison us and hang us if we broke the law, the law requiring that all Indian children go to school.*

*I screamed and cried when they took our Rabbit away. After that day, I was never the same. Neither was my husband.*

*We were promised that Rabbit would return every summer for a visit. They lied. We saw him once. They had cut his beautiful hair and had forbidden him from speaking our language or practicing our religion. They had told him he would burn forever after death if he disobeyed. They had burned his clothes and had made him wear an ugly uniform. They had even changed his name to Randal Smith.*

*He cried and begged us not to let them take him from us again, but the officers had guns, and we were afraid that they would kill our son if we disobeyed them. After that, we never saw Rabbit again.*

*I wept for many moons. Talks to Buffalo spent more and more time away from me. He came home drunk on the liquor he bought from the shady white men that preyed on our people on the borders of the reservation, tempting them with hard liquors to forget their pain and loss.*

*My husband stopped hunting and fishing. I found it hard to tend the garden. We came to rely on the government rations. The summers and winters went by in misery. Our house fell apart around us, but my husband and I no longer cared.*

*One day the white men came looking for Rabbit. I was confused.*

*"He's at school," I said.*

*"He ran away," one of the men said.*

*At first, I was happy. I imagined Rabbit free of the white men. I hoped he might find his way back to me. My happiness did not last long. When the white men said that Rabbit had misused a nun and was a fugitive of the law, I knew they were lying. Dread filled my heart. My sweet Rabbit was doomed.*

*That summer, Talks to Buffalo participated in the blood ritual of the Sun Dance. I prayed daily. But when the winter came and went and we still heard nothing of our Rabbit, we fell into despair.*

*I don't know how we lived. We might as well have been dead. Talks to Buffalo turned to his drink. I wanted to kill myself but the thought that Rabbit might one day need me prevented me from following through with my plans.*

*Talks to Buffalo died three summers ago. Before he died, he told me to sell the white buffalo hide, so I could have food to live. I told him it is against our ways to sell a white buffalo hide. He said I should do it anyway. I told him it was the only thing I had left of him and the happy times.*

*I would die today but for one thing: Rabbit may need me someday.*

Karen looked up and closed the book. "That's the end."

"How sad," Tanya said. "The mistreatment of your people needs to be more public. It should be taught in schools."

"Instead, they teach your children about a friendly relationship between pilgrims and Indians. But it wasn't like that."

"History is white-washed," Ellen murmured with tears in her eyes.

"We have to make things right for Crow Woman," Sue said. "If the second set of remains are proven to be those of Rabbit, we should bury him here on the property with a special crossover ceremony."

"What do you think, Karen?" Tanya asked.

"I don't want to get my hopes up," she said. "Let's take this one step at a time. First, we need to find out if you've really found Rabbit. Those remains could belong to someone else."

Ellen left the circle of protection and crossed the room to the old bench where the dusty white buffalo hide lay. Gingerly, she reached out and touched the fur. As had happened before, a jolt of electricity shot up her arm.

"Rabbit's spirit is in this fur," Ellen said. "I can feel it."

"He and his mother should dwell with the rest of our ancestors at the Badger-Two Medicine," Karen said. "They're trapped here because of the trauma they endured in life."

"I hope we can help them," Tanya said.

"Me, too," Karen said.

CHAPTER THIRTEEN

# Change

Saturday evening, Ellen decided to eat her dinner alone in her room at Glacier Park Lodge. She made an excuse to Tanya and Sue about needing to elevate her ankle, but what was really bothering her was the story of Crow Woman. Ellen ordered room service and then sat in front of the television to wait for her meal.

Even *Downton Abbey* couldn't pull Ellen from her racing thoughts. It wasn't just the horrendous treatment that Crow Woman and her people had endured at the hands of the U.S. government. It was also the loneliness and despair that had dominated the woman's life. When Ellen imagined a lonely, heart-broken widow waiting for her child to return, she saw her own future.

Of course, Ellen's children weren't dead at the bottom of some river. But Crow Woman hadn't known about her son's demise. She had gone from having her son there in her life every single day, as important as the food she ate and the air she breathed, to not having him at all.

Ellen felt guilty for comparing herself to Crow Woman, for feeling sorry for herself when she lived in luxury and had wonderful children and friends. Even so, she longed for the days when she and her children and husband lived under the same roof, the happiest time of her life.

Now, her children rarely called. Nolan was busy with his new residency and his new girlfriend. Lane had graduated and was working his first real job in Austin. And Alison was finishing up her graduate degree. When she called them, she felt as if she were interfering, detaining them from something more important. They didn't need her anymore. But she needed them.

Thank goodness for Tanya and Sue and for their willingness to immerse themselves in these paranormal investigations. However, Ellen dreaded the possibility that this could be their last adventure. Tanya nearly hadn't come. And Sue was only interested in the property because she wanted a vacation home. She'd had dozens of requests on her blog to investigate haunted properties. Neither she nor Tanya had been interested in pursuing those leads. Sue and Tanya didn't need to be a part of Ghost Healers, Inc., anymore. For whatever reason, they were ready to move on, which left Ellen wondering what she would do with her life.

And then there was Brian. He'd asked her to travel the world with him and then accused her of holding him at arm's length. He'd been right. She hadn't intended to keep her distance. She'd wanted to love him as fully as—and perhaps even more fully than—she'd loved Paul. Why couldn't she? Why couldn't she let go of whatever it was that was holding her back?

She gazed through the tall windows at the lovely mountain view, where the sun was setting in all its brilliance. Ellen wondered if the simple answer to her question was that she was afraid of change. Rich Falcon had said that the one constant in life was change. The mountains were constantly cut and reshaped by the shrinking glaciers, melting ice, and tumbling water. Nothing ever stayed the same, not even the earth. So why should she?

She took out her phone to call Brian but was interrupted by a knock at her door. It was room service with her salad.

Maybe she'd call Brian another time.

The following morning, Ellen still didn't feel like leaving her room. She made an excuse to get out of breakfast with Sue and Tanya, even though she knew that isolating herself from her friends would only make her feel worse. She felt like she needed someone to tell her what to do. She felt as if she'd fallen overboard and was sinking to the bottom of a river.

She took out her phone, intending to call Brian, but as she scrolled through her contacts, her eyes fell upon Eduardo Mankiller, one of the psychics she and her friends had worked with in Tulsa. She hadn't spoken to him in nearly four years, but she clicked on his number and called him.

"Oh my, Ellen! I was just thinking about you!" he said into the phone.

Ellen laughed. "I bet you say that to everyone who calls."

"Is that shade you're throwing at me? You know me better than that!"

"I'm just teasing," she said. "How have you been?"

He told her about his most recent project with Carrie French and Miss Margaret Myrtle involving an old building that had served as a flophouse during the 1800's.

Ellen told him what she and Sue and Tanya were doing in Montana.

"Are you asking me to fly up there?" Eduardo said. "Because you know that I would in a heartbeat."

"No, though I wouldn't stop you if you wanted to," she said. "I just think we've done all we can at this point."

"I get it."

"I called because I was wondering if you'd do me the favor of reading my cards over the phone. I could Paypal you the fee."

"Of course, girlfriend! You know I'm always happy to be of service. Let me shuffle my cards while you think on your question. Is there anything in particular you want to know?"

She sucked in her lips and fought back tears. "Not really. I guess I'm looking for guidance. Where do I go from here—you know what I mean?"

"I know exactly what you mean. Okay, I'm cutting the cards, and I'm laying them out. Oh, yes. This is very clear to me, Ellen."

"Lay it on me. What do you see?"

"The first card is about intuition. You haven't been listening to yours. You've been avoiding it. Embrace it, Ellen, Stop fighting it. You know what to do. You just aren't listening to yourself."

"I suppose that's fair."

"The next card is about sacrifice. It's good that you want to sacrifice your time and energy for others, but you can't do it at the price of your own well-being. You need to take time for yourself, to save yourself. You know the saying about when you're on a plane, you have to put the oxygen mask on yourself first, right?"

"Right."

"And the last card is about awakenings, about a new rite of passage, about a death and a rebirth. It's time for you to let something go so that you can begin a new chapter of your life."

Tears flowed down Ellen's cheeks. He wasn't telling her anything she didn't already know. She had to let go of her past and embrace her future, but, damn, if it wasn't the hardest thing she'd ever had to do.

"Thank you, Eduardo. That's just what I needed to hear."

Instead of phoning Brian, Ellen decided to write to him. In the letter, she was completely raw with him, admitting that she didn't know what she was doing, but she knew that she needed to do something. She couldn't go on like this. She loved him and didn't want to lose him, but she had to take things slow. She asked if he could give her another chance, even if it would take her a while to allow him to be any closer to her than arm's length.

Before she could change her mind, she went to the business office downstairs, bought an envelope and postage, and dropped the letter into the mail. As soon as she did, she felt much better.

She was about to knock on Tanya's door when her phone rang. It was Father Gonzales.

"I don't have time to talk," he said. "I'm about to serve mass. But I was wondering if you and Sue and Tanya might be able to come by the rectory later, perhaps around three o'clock? I have news, but it's mixed, and I'd like to discuss it in person."

"Of course, Father," Ellen said. "We'll see you at the rectory at three."

Ellen arrived with her friends by taxi to the rectory at three o'clock sharp. Father Gonzales welcomed them inside, to the sitting area where the two of them had spent the night after falling overboard the *Sinopah*. Ellen took her wingback chair as Sue and Tanya shared the couch facing the empty fireplace.

"Can I get you ladies some coffee or tea?" Father Gonzales offered.

The ladies declined, having just eaten a late lunch together at the Rock-N-Roll Bakery.

"But I have something for you," Sue said. "This is the best cinnamon roll you'll ever eat."

Father Gonzales accepted the bag from the bakery before taking a seat in the wingback opposite Ellen. "It's my favorite. Thank you. I'll have it for breakfast tomorrow."

"Out with it," Ellen finally said. "We're dying to know what you've heard."

Father Gonzales blushed. "First of all, the medical examiner confirmed that one of the legs belonging to the second body is indeed shorter than the other."

Sue clapped her hands. "I knew it!"

Father Gonzales glanced toward the hall. "I expect Father O'Brien's naptime is over."

Sue covered her mouth as the blood rushed to her face. "I'm sorry. I didn't know."

He waved a hand at her. "No worries. I think I can still hear him snoring, actually."

"Why is this mixed news, Father?" Tanya asked.

"Well, apparently it's quite common for people to have one leg longer than the other. Officer Jackson told me that it happens in forty to seventy percent of the human population."

"Oh, no," Ellen groaned. She felt completely deflated. "Then we've proved nothing."

"The good news is that the discrepancy in leg length is usually unnoticeable," the priest said. "The fact that Rabbit's was severe enough to affect his walking might set him apart. And the medical examiner did concede that the discrepancy in the case of the remains was severe. He also said that the remains were of a male who was approximately seventeen years of age when he died, and that the bones appeared to have been at the bottom of the river for at least one hundred years. This is all consistent with the body belonging to Rabbit."

"Well, then!" Sue said, a little too loudly again. She covered her mouth. "Sorry."

"The problem is that the authorities aren't willing to accept the results of a paranormal investigation or a memoir handwritten in Piegan as evidence that Rabbit had such a condition. Officer Jackson says the medical examiner has documented the second body as a John Doe."

Ellen wanted to cry.

"They accepted the letters of Father Galdas in identifying Sister Alma," Sue pointed out.

"They had the rosary," the priest said.

"Someone else could have jumped in the river with Alma's rosary," Sue argued.

Father Gonzales nodded. "It's unfair. Completely unfair."

"Well, *we* know the truth," Tanya said. "Isn't that good enough?"

"I don't know," Father Gonzales said. "Didn't you say you wanted to bury Rabbit at his home with his parents? I'm not sure if you or anyone will be able to claim the body. The ME won't release the remains to just anyone."

"What about Sister Alma?" Sue asked.

"She's being released to Holy Family Mission in a few days," he said.

"There's got to be a way," Tanya muttered.

"Us knowing the truth isn't good enough by a longshot." Ellen shifted in her chair. "Not if we want to convince Sidney Longfellow that he's a descendant of the Blackfeet. Not if we want the white buffalo hide to find its rightful owner. Not if we want Rabbit and Crow Woman to find peace."

"Mr. Longfellow may surprise us," Tanya said. "Maybe he'll be open to the idea."

Sue shook her head. "It would be too much of a conflict of interest for him to both accept his heritage and litigate for drilling rights. If Karen's right and all he cares about is money, he won't accept the hide."

"A letter from the medical examiner might have changed that," Ellen said. "But without the authorities on our side, I think it's a lost cause."

"We'll just have to find a way to convince him," Tanya said. "Come on, guys. You dragged me out here for a reason. Don't tell me you're giving up this easily."

Ellen wiped the tears from her eyes. "What choice do we have?"

"We should at least reach out to Mr. Longfellow," Tanya said. "Shouldn't we? We can't not give it a try."

Sue lifted a finger. "Maybe it's time we went back to the French Quarter."

"I don't know." It seemed like a waste of time to Ellen.

"Hear me out." Sue sat up on the end of the couch. "You said the white buffalo fur shocked you, right?"

"So?"

"Well, if Sidney is the rightful owner of it, wouldn't it shock him, too?"

"Maybe," Ellen said. She lifted her brows. She was reminded of something the white buffalo had said to her in her dream. "I suppose it's our best chance. What do you think, Tanya?"

"I'm game, but only if we take the train."

Ellen turned to Sue.

"The train it is," Sue said.

Ellen sighed. "Now we just need to convince the tribe to let us take the fur with us."

The next day at breakfast, as they sat at a table in the lodge restaurant overlooking the beautiful mountains, Ellen, Sue, and Tanya called Karen Murray to update her on what they'd been told by the Jesuit priest and to ask her opinion about their taking the white buffalo skin to New Orleans.

Over the speaker on Sue's phone, Karen said, "Chief Eric Old Person would be the one to ask, but I can tell you now, he won't allow it. The white buffalo is too sacred to our people, and, no offense, but we don't know you well enough to trust you with it."

"I understand," Sue said. "What if I go forward with my plans to buy the property? You did say that I would become its custodian."

"It's custodian, but not its owner," Karen said. "The chief would never allow it to be taken off the reservation by anyone but a member of our tribe."

"Could *you* come with us?" Ellen asked.

Karen's laughter carried over the speaker. "Not everyone has the luxury of travelling at their leisure. Some of us have to work for a living."

"Ouch," Ellen whispered.

"Speaking of which," Karen added, "I should get back to mine."

"Before you go, is there anyone you can think of that might be willing to accompany us?" Sue asked her.

"Not off the top of my head. If I think of someone, I'll let you know."

They ended the call and sat quietly for a moment, allowing the disappointment to settle in.

Then Sue lifted a finger. "What about Rich Falcon, our tour guide? He owns his own business. I bet if we offered to pay him each day for more than he could make otherwise, he'd agree. Don't you think?"

Ellen and Tanya exchanged smiles.

"Good idea, Sue!" Tanya said.

"You'd be surprised how often I'm told that," Sue said with a grin.

CHAPTER FOURTEEN

# Return to the French Quarter

After Chief Eric Old Person agreed to allow Rich Falcon to take the white buffalo hide from Talks to Buffalo Lodge off reservation, Rich took the fur to a fellow tribal member to have it cleaned while Ellen, Sue, and Tanya made their travel arrangements. The ladies decided to keep one of their rooms at Glacier Park Lodge, so they wouldn't have to take everything with them. They also hoped to return within the week, even though the better part of their time would be spent on the train.

Ellen wasn't excited about spending two days and three hours on the train to New Orleans, but she supposed it was better for both Tanya and the buffalo skin. Even if they'd flown first class, they would have had to stuff the hide in the overhead bin or check it with the luggage, and neither of those options seemed safe. On the train, there was plenty of room for Rich to drape the fur beside him in the large, comfy seat.

Fortunately, a new mystery novel kept Ellen occupied. By the time she'd finished it, they were only a few minutes outside of New Orleans.

Sue had managed to book their old room at the Inn on Ursulines—the one with the two queen beds. Rich stayed in a smaller room with a twin bed. He seemed to be happy because it was on the top floor and had a nice view of the French Quarter. It was late Wednesday night when they arrived and, since they had eaten on the train, they went to bed, because the morning would come early for them.

Ellen, Sue, and Tanya met Rich Falcon downstairs in the lobby at eight o'clock the next morning. Rich was wearing the white buffalo fur like a cape over his button up, long-sleeved shirt and blue jeans. The buffalo head lay on his upper back like a large hood.

"Good morning," he said to them with a nod.

"Good morning," they said back.

"Did you sleep okay?" Ellen asked him.

"I'm not used to all the city noise," he admitted, "but I eventually fell asleep."

"We need caffeine," Sue said. "There's a bakery we love that's not far from here. They have excellent coffee and pastries."

They took a cab to their favorite bakery a block away from their condos on Chartres Street. From there, they paid a brief visit to Maria Nunnery, the woman they had hired to manage the property.

Ellen was surprised at how well their old friend looked. She no longer had a missing front tooth, her long hair had been cut into a stylish bob, and she was wearing makeup and fashionable clothes.

After introducing Maria to Rich Falcon, Ellen and her friends filled her in on what they'd been doing in Montana. Then Maria told them what she'd been up to. They were pleased to learn that her daughter, Cecilia, was in the process of having Maria's house rebuilt. The house had been destroyed years ago during Hurricane Katrina, and it had been Maria's dream to return to her home one day.

"Best of all, Jamar got a job," Maria said, "He works for a construction firm. He's there now."

"That's wonderful news," Sue said.

"Does he still write poetry?" Ellen asked.

"Not as much anymore, but some."

"I bet he's excited about the house, too," Tanya said.

"He sure is," Maria said with a bright smile.

"Will you continue to work with us after you move?" Sue asked.

"If you'll have me," Maria said. "And, since you'll be able to rent or sell my unit, you can afford to give me a raise."

"True!" Ellen said. "Very true!"

Ellen referred to the units as condos, but they were really apartments, as the tenants rented rather than owned. But it had always been her plan to convert them into properties that encouraged home ownership in the French Quarter. They were in the process of working out the details with the two families that lived there.

From Chartres Street, Ellen and her party took a cab to downtown New Orleans, to a modern high-rise office building where Solonex was located on the twelfth floor. They arrived at their ten-o'clock appointment fifteen minutes early but only waited in the posh waiting room for a few minutes before a young woman entered and asked them to follow her to see Mr. Longfellow.

A tall, well-built man in his late seventies or early eighties stood up from behind a desk and greeted each of them as they entered, offering them his hand and then cups of coffee, which they declined. Then he asked them to take a seat as he returned to a chair behind the desk.

Photos on his desk and on the walls pictured him with a lovely wife, a son, and a daughter, both with families of their own. A small crucifix hung over a degree from Louisiana State University from the late sixties. As he smiled at them patiently from behind his desk and said, "How can I help you good people?", he didn't strike Ellen as the unfeeling, greedy man Karen Murray had made him out to be.

"We're here to help *you*, Mr. Longfellow," Sue said.

"Please call me Sidney. I've been officially retired now for over a decade, but I like to keep an eye on things from time to time. I'm only here today because your message sounded urgent. I must say, however, I still have no idea as to why you're here. I'm afraid my business ventures are behind me. If you are looking for an investor, you might want to talk to my son."

"We're not here because of a business venture," Ellen said. "It's actually a personal matter involving your biological grandparents."

"Biological grandparents?" he repeated.

"Which of your parents was adopted?" Sue asked. "Was it your father?"

"What makes you think either of my parents was adopted? I'm afraid you have the wrong man. I'm sorry to disappoint you. It appears you came all this way for nothing."

Ellen exchanged looks of confusion with her friends. Even Rich Falcon couldn't look more stunned.

"We have proof," Ellen said. "Bodies found recently in the Two-Medicine River near Holy Family Mission Church have a 75% DNA match to your DNA."

Sue lifted her finger. "That means…"

"I'm afraid you don't have your facts straight." He stood up, as a way of indicating to them that the meeting was over. "Neither of my parents was adopted. Someone is pulling either your leg or mine."

Ellen stood up, too, and placed her hand on the white buffalo robe, which immediately pulsed electricity through her arm. "No one is pulling anyone's leg. If you'd just give us a chance to explain. We've come all this way to give you this rare and sacred white buffalo hide because it's your birthright. It belonged to your grandfather, Rabbit, and to his father, Talks to Buffalo."

Sidney's face flushed red. "Is this some kind of gimmick? Did the Blackfeet send you here to trick me into dropping my lawsuit?"

"We would never trick you," Rich Falcon said, "unlike the U.S. government."

"You *are* a Blackfoot. I knew it. I don't believe this. Shame on you. This is low. The tribe and the government have been sitting on this issue for nearly forty years, and now this. I would like you to leave, please—right now. Or I'll call security."

"Couldn't you just touch the fur and see for yourself?" Ellen asked him.

Sidney picked up the receiver on his desk phone and punched a number before saying, "I need security up here."

"We're leaving," Sue said. "There's no need for that."

Ellen followed Rich Falcon and her friends from the office and to the elevators near the lobby.

"How disappointing," Tanya murmured as she pushed the down button.

"This was pointless," Rich Falcon complained. "I had a feeling it would be."

"No," Sue said. "This isn't over."

The elevators opened to reveal two security guards. After the guards stepped out, Ellen and her party stepped in and took the elevator down.

"That was close," Tanya said.

Ellen crossed her arms and turned to her friends. "I have an idea."

"I'm glad to hear I don't have to carry all the weight around here," Sue said before adding, "I meant that figuratively, of course. Let's hear it, Ellen."

"I think we should visit the Voodoo Spiritual Temple and ask High Priestess Isabel for help."

"The what?" Rich Falcon asked with a nod of his head.

"I'm game," Tanya said with a smile.

A half hour later, Ellen and her party arrived via taxi to the Voodoo Spiritual Temple on North Rampart, on the edge of the French Quarter. Ellen led the way inside the shop full of voodoo dolls, gris-gris bags, and other paraphernalia and was pleasantly surprised to see Priestess Isabel standing beside the counter with a can of Sprite in her hand. A young woman was with her, sitting on a stool near the cash register.

"Well, hello friends," Isabel said. "It's been a while."

The high priestess didn't appear a day older than she had looked the last time they'd seen her, over three years ago, which should make her about eighty. Her short curly hair and bright smile were exactly as Ellen remembered them.

"Hello, Priestess Isabel," Ellen said. "May I introduce our friend, Rich Falcon of Blackfeet Nation?"

"Welcome to my humble place," Isabel said.

"It's a pleasure to meet you," Rich said with a nod.

"I see you brought a friend with you," Isabel added.

Ellen could tell from Isabel's line of vision that the priestess wasn't referring to Sue or Tanya. Could she see Rabbit in the white buffalo hide?

Sue and Ellen told Isabel what they were doing in New Orleans, recounting everything that had happened in Montana, including the dream Ellen had had of the white buffalo and their recent encounter with Sidney Longfellow.

"You've been busy," she said with a laugh.

A customer came in, so the priestess excused herself to talk with the young woman. The priestess handed a bottle to the assistant at the cash register, who took over from there.

Isabel turned to Ellen. "Did you come to throw the bones?"

"Do you have time?" Ellen asked.

"Follow me, my friends."

Isabel led them through her tiny, cluttered back office and into a courtyard filled with trees, herbs, and other plants. The courtyard had a table with two chairs at its center and was bordered by raised beds lined with pavers that served as extra seating.

Isabel sat in one of the two chairs. "Who wants to throw first?"

"I will," Sue said as she sat across from the high priestess.

The table was covered with a green fibrous cloth with yellow markings. The bones and shells lay scattered on the cloth. Sue, knowing what to do, scooped up the bones and shells, shook them in her hands, and asked, "How can we help Rabbit and Crow Woman?" Then she dropped the bones and shells on the cloth. One shell fell off the table.

"Do you see an x on that one?" Isabel asked Tanya of the one that had fallen, since Tanya was closest to it.

"No," Tanya said.

"Then we can ignore that one," the priestess said. "Now, let's look and see what we have here."

Isabel looked over each bone and shell, shaking her head.

"What is it?" Sue asked.

"I don't think this spirit knows the answer to your question," the priestess said. "But I think I'm channeling someone more powerful—maybe a Loa."

"Really?" Ellen asked from where she hovered over Sue.

"The placement of this bone means trickery," Isabel said. "And this one here suggests a party. I think this message has something to do with the masquerade benefit going on at the Federal Ballroom tonight."

"The Federal Ballroom?" Sue repeated. "Where's that?"

"It's a seven-minute car ride from here," Isabel said. "If I remember correctly, it's being put on by the New Blue Foundation to raise money for autism. I think the bones are telling me that this Sidney Longfellow will be there."

Sue took out her phone and did a search. She tapped on the top result. "It's five hundred dollars a ticket."

"Jiminy Crickets," Rich Falcon said. "That's a lot of money."

"The dress code is black tie only, masks required," Sue said. "Oh, and it says here that Sidney Longfellow is a major benefactor of New Blue Foundation!"

"Oh, Isabela, you rock!" Ellen cried gleefully.

Tanya lifted her palms in the air. "It sounds like we're going shopping."

"You ladies need to visit The Red Carpet," the priestess said. "It's a boutique in the Garden District."

"Did you see that in the bones?" Sue teased.

"I didn't need to," Isabel replied with a smile.

# CHAPTER FIFTEEN

# The Masquerade Ball

Once they reached the Garden District, Ellen and her friends had the cab driver drop Rich Falcon at a tuxedo rental to be fitted. Then they headed a few more blocks to The Red Carpet, a cute boutique on Magazine Street.

"This should be fun," Tanya said as they climbed from the cab and paid the driver.

"Speak for yourself," Sue said. "These places never have anything in my size."

The gray and red shop looked small and crowded by the larger buildings beside it. Ellen worried there might not be enough of a selection to meet their needs. But when she walked inside and saw the length of it, with gorgeous gowns lining every square inch of the walls on either side and hanging from racks on the floor, she felt giddy with excitement.

Sue sat down on a red velvet sofa. "You two go ahead. There's no reason for us *all* to go to the ball. The most important thing is for you to get Rich Falcon and his buffalo fur in contact with Sidney Longfellow."

"Sue, don't be like that," Tanya said. "We'll find something for you."

"May I help you ladies?"

A woman as large as Sue emerged from a back room. She was a young black woman dressed to the nines in glitz and glamor. Her royal blue gown hugged her hour-glass shape. The dress was floor-length and sparkled with iridescent beads. The neckline was low and flattering. She looked incredible.

Sue's chin nearly hit the floor. "Wow. That dress is stunning on you."

"Thank you."

"Can you help me find something like that?" Sue asked.

"I'm sure I can," the young woman said. "Follow me."

While the store clerk helped Sue, Ellen and Tanya combed the racks. Ellen had never seen so many gorgeous gowns in one place.

"What do you think of this?" Tanya held up a silver fringed gown by Mac Duggal.

"It's lovely. Try it on."

"Or what about this one?" Tanya held up a second gown by Mac Duggal with an asymmetric neckline. It was chiffon with a red blossom print on a light gray background and a sheer set-in bell sleeve.

"Oh, my," Ellen said. "That one's nice, too. Try them both on."

Not long after Tanya had left for the dressing room, Ellen found a gown by Jovani made of a soft and stretchy navy-blue lace. It had a wide shoulder neckline with a very subtle scallop. Because Ellen didn't like her upper arms, she was glad it had three-quarter set-in sleeves. The gown was fitted, but not too fitted, at the bodice and hips and flowed in a sheath style to the floor. She hoped it looked as good on as it did on the rack.

In the fitting room, Ellen climbed into the dress and studied herself in the full-length mirror. She couldn't be more pleased. The navy blue went well with her complexion and her dark blonde hair. The fabric hugged her without showing any rolls of fat. And the length of the gown elongated her, making her look less round. She stepped from the dressing room to see if her friends agreed that she'd found the right gown.

Tanya was in the main showroom in front of a three-way mirror donning the gray chiffon dress with the red blossom print. It was tied at the waist with a thin black belt.

"You look beautiful," Ellen said.

Tanya looked up as Ellen approached the mirror. "Oh, Ellen. You do, too. I love that on you."

Just then, Sue emerged wearing an off-shoulder Tiffany in gold and black brocade with angel sleeves and a drop waist. She looked like a mermaid princess.

"Oh, wow, Sue!" Ellen said. "You look amazing."

"You really do!" Tanya said.

"She cinched my waist, so I can't really breathe, but I don't mind." Then she said, "You two look amazing, too. I'd say we hit the jackpot. Now we just need jewelry and shoes."

"And masks," Tanya said.

Once they were in the cab with their bags and heading back to the tuxedo rental to pick up Rich, Ellen noticed that Sue was crying.

"Sue?" she asked gently from the front passenger's seat. "Are you okay?"

"I really didn't think I'd find something that would make me feel beautiful," she said. "I know I'm being silly. It's just a dress."

"You're not being silly," Tanya said.

"I wish my mother could have seen it on me," Sue said. "I miss her so much."

"I'm sure she's looking down on you with pride," Ellen said.

"I wouldn't go that far," Sue said with a forced laugh.

"*I* would." Tanya put an arm around her friend in the backseat.

Rich Falcon looked handsome in his sharp tuxedo, with the white buffalo fur draped across his shoulders like a cape. He wore his white hair loose from its usual ponytail and combed straight back. Ellen thought he looked much more attractive with his hair that way, resembling Lucius Malfoy in the *Harry Potter* movies.

"Golly," she said when she saw him as she emerged from the elevator in the lobby of the Inn on Ursulines. "Don't you look nice."

"I feel like the luckiest man alive," he said. "To be escorting three beautiful ladies to a fancy party. Wowza. Those dresses look incredible on you."

"What do you think of our masks?" Tanya held hers in front of her face. It was silver and red, like her gown, but in a harlequin pattern with silver lace trim and a red handle. They'd all opted to wear the kind that one held up to one's face rather than risk ruining hair and makeup with elastic bands or ribbons.

Ellen's mask was covered in white lace and pearl trim and had a white feather on one side. Sue's was gold with black trim, black beads dangling along the bottom, and black feathers all along the top.

"Very nice," Rich said.

"Here's one for you/" Ellen handed him a plain black one with an elastic band.

"Thank you," he said with a nod. "Are we ready, then?"

They had decided to splurge by ordering a limo to transport them to and from the benefit. It seemed wrong to arrive in a taxicab looking so fancy. The limo was already waiting for them at the curb.

The former federal reserve bank that was now the Federal Ballroom was an impressive white stone building with a red awning and floor-to-ceiling colonial-style windows. Inside, Ellen and her friends found massively high coffered white ceilings with two rows of tall white pillars separating the dancefloor from the round tables on either side. The pillars were made more beautiful by spotlights that illuminated them from their base, creating a dramatic ambience. On the opposite side of the long dancefloor was a stage where band members were setting up. Elegantly dressed people were making their way to the tables on the outskirts of the room.

As Ellen and her friends searched for a table, they passed by the buffet stations where they saw Caesar salad, shrimp and grits, crawfish etouffee, pasta primavera, chicken and sausage gumbo, roast beef debris with mashed potatoes, a beef tenderloin carving station, a fried turkey carving station, a roasted pig carving station with pork tenderloins and jambalaya, alligator sausage, crawfish sausage, shrimp sausage, grilled chicken breast, grilled catfish, bananas foster, coffee and beignets, and French bread pudding with rum sauce—all catered by Capdeboscq.

"My, my, my," Sue said. "This may prove to be our best trip yet."

They eventually found a round table for six in the furthest corner, off to the right of the stage. It was practically hidden behind a speaker system and a pillar, which was fortunate since the plan was to keep themselves and the buffalo fur inconspicuous, so as not to alert Sidney Longfellow of their presence. Rich Falcon draped the fur on the sixth chair, out of view, and waited with it while the ladies went through the food stations. When they returned with their plates full, Rich left for his turn.

"Have you seen him yet?" Ellen asked her friends of Sidney Longfellow.

"Not yet," Sue said. "Have you, Tanya?"

"No, but there are a lot of people here. I'm sure he's here somewhere."

"Remember the plan," Sue said. "One of us needs to get him on the dancefloor while another of us discreetly goes onto the floor with Rich."

"Who's going to dance with whom?" Ellen asked before taking a bite of her shrimp and grits.

"*You* better ask Mr. Longfellow to dance," Sue said to Ellen. "Tanya won't have the guts to do it, and he might turn me down."

"Oh, stop," I said. "But I'm happy to do it."

"Just remember to hold up your mask," Sue said.

"I will, I promise."

"And Tanya, why don't you go with Rich?" Sue suggested. "You're less memorable than I am and are less likely to draw attention."

"Excuse me?" Tanya asked as her face turned white.

"I meant that as a compliment," Sue said. "People remember me everywhere I go because of my size. You blend in with the rest of the beautiful people."

"Please stop, Sue," Ellen said. "You know you look beautiful tonight. You said so yourself."

"You're right," she said. "I'm just not used to feeling good about myself."

"So, what will you do while we're on the dancefloor?" Tanya asked Sue.

"I'll be on the sidelines waiting to intervene once Sidney Longfellow realizes that he's been shocked by the white buffalo."

Rich returned to their table, so they ladies went over the details of their plan again with him.

"You're sure it wouldn't be easier for me to bump into him in the men's room?" Rich asked.

"You can't hang out there all evening waiting on his bladder," Ellen said. "Besides, we want to be there when it happens."

"I suppose we *could* hide out in the men's room," Sue said with a laugh. "We've done worse."

"Let's just stick with the original plan," Tanya said.

Suddenly, Sue said, "Oh, no."

"What's wrong?" Tanya asked with dread on her face.

Ellen followed the line of Sue's vision and was shocked to see Brian sitting at a table with a beautiful woman less than half his age. His gray eyes sparkled beneath his thick, dark brows, and his dazzling smile, caused by the gorgeous young thing beside him, made Ellen frown.

"Oh, God," Ellen said, bringing her hand to her stomach. "I think I'm going to be sick."

"Breathe, Ellen," Sue said. "You have to stay focused. Remember why we're here."

Tanya turned to see what the hullaballoo was all about. "What is *he* doing here?"

"Who *is* he?" Rich asked.

"Ellen's ex-boyfriend," Sue explained.

The phrase *ex-boyfriend* made Ellen's stomach clench into a knot. "Excuse me for a moment. I'll be right back."

Ellen lifted her mask to her face and crossed the ballroom in search of a restroom. Once she was inside the ladies' room, Ellen took a good look at herself in the mirror. Why was it that when she finally mustered up the nerve to confess her love to Brian—in writing, no less—he decided to move on? The universe must enjoy taking pleasure in its cruel, ironic tricks.

She found a tissue and blew her nose, fixed her makeup, and washed her hands. She straightened her dress, took another look at herself from all sides, and then took a deep breath. Tonight wasn't about her. It was about helping Rabbit and Crow Woman. She needed to get over herself, pull up her big girl panties, and get to work. Lifting her mask to her face, she left the ladies' room full of resolve.

Back in the ballroom, the band had begun to play, and a few couples were on the dancefloor waltzing to the slow, romantic melody. Ellen avoided looking across the room at Brian's table as she made a beeline for her own.

"Are you okay?" Tanya asked.

Ellen took her seat and drank down the last of her wine. "Absolutely. Has anyone had a Sidney sighting yet?"

"He's standing in line for a drink," Sue said. "This might be a good time to grab him, while he's away from his wife and friends."

Ellen lifted her mask to her face. "Ready then?"

Her friends nodded.

Trembling a little, Ellen headed for the drink line, where Sidney Longfellow was waiting.

When she reached him, she said, "Excuse me, Mr. Longfellow. On behalf of the New Blue Foundation, I'd like to thank you again for your generous support of people with autism."

"Oh, thank you," he said. "It's my pleasure. You've put on a beautiful event tonight. You should be proud."

"Thank you," Ellen said, feeling guilty over her lie. Reminding herself that it was for a good cause, she said, "Speaking of which, would you do me the honor of dancing with me? We'd like to get a photo for the website."

"Oh, in that case, of course."

He led her onto the dancefloor, where she searched for Tanya and Rich, Instead, she saw Brian dancing with his cute little girlfriend.

"Ugh," she said without thinking, as she held her mask to her face with one hand and held Sidney's hand with the other.

He put a hand to her waist to lead her in the waltz while asking, "Is something the matter?"

"Oh, I just saw my ex-boyfriend with another woman—a girl, actually. She can't be more than twenty."

Sidney frowned. "Oh, dear. I'm sorry to hear that. Anyway, it's obvious that it's *his* loss."

"Thank you, Mr. Longfellow."

"Now, let's see. Where is your photographer?"

"He should be coming over any moment now."

Ellen noticed Tanya and Rich had finally made it onto the floor. The white buffalo fur shone brightly in the otherwise dim ballroom. It was difficult to keep it conspicuous, despite the crowd. Ellen pulled Sidney toward her, so that his back was to the other couple.

"Trying to avoid him?" he asked.

"Yes. If you don't mind."

"If I weren't married to the most wonderful woman in the world, I'd offer to kiss you, to make him jealous."

Ellen laughed. "Bullocks for me, then."

"Are you English?"

"Oh, no. I just read a lot of novels and watch a lot of *Downton Abbey*."

It was Sidney's turn to laugh. "How charming."

There were a lot of couples on the floor, now, and Ellen was worried that Rich wouldn't be able to successfully maneuver through them to Ellen's side before the song ended. To help them along, and at the risk of making a fool of herself, she said, "Oh, please, go backward. Let me lead. I don't want him to see me."

She pushed Sidney though the other dancing couples, bumping into one or two along the way, but he took it like a sport, until, at last, he bumped into the fur of the white buffalo.

He turned around to see Rich Falcon and Tanya standing behind him.

"Did you feel it?" Ellen asked him as she dropped her mask from her face.

"You?" Sidney said angrily, once he'd put together what was happening. "I can't believe it! Just when I thought you'd gone as low as anyone could possibly go."

"Ellen?"

Ellen responded to the call of her name to find it had come from Brian. He stood with his date on the dancefloor with his eyes wide and his mouth hanging open.

"I thought you were in Montana," he said.

"You know this imposter, Brian?" Sidney cried in disbelief.

"She's my…friend," he faltered after glancing at his date.

"She's despicable, that's what she is," Sidney said before he stormed off.

Ellen followed her friends from the dancefloor, feeling mortified and heartbroken. Hadn't Sidney felt the shock of the hide? And, if he hadn't, had she and her friends gotten everything wrong?

"Ellen, wait," Brian said as he grabbed her by the arm at the edge of the dancefloor. "Can we at least talk for a minute?"

His date had returned to their table.

Tears flooded Ellen's eyes. "What good would it do? I was clearly too late."

"Too late? Too late for what?" he asked.

"With my letter," she said. "You've moved on."

"What letter?"

Suddenly, it dawned on her that he hadn't received her letter. But would it have made a difference? His date was so young and sexy and sweet. If he was capable of dating someone like her, why would he want Ellen?

"Never mind. If you do receive it, just rip it up."

Ellen pulled her arm free and quickly returned to her table, where her friends sat moping over their failure.

Without sitting down, Ellen said, "Let's get out of here."

She hurried off to the curb, ahead of her friends, where she phoned their limo.

Brian caught up to her as her friends were still trying to exit the crowded entrance.

"Ellen, please talk to me," he said.

"I can't," she said through her tears. "Another time, okay?"

His date called from the entrance, "Brian? Aren't you coming inside?" Then she noticed Ellen, who had quickly covered her face with her mask, to hide her tear-stained cheeks. "Oh, hello, ma'am. I didn't mean to interrupt."

Ellen inwardly groaned. Aloud, she said, "That's alright. We're done here."

The limo pulled up just in time to save Ellen from further embarrassment. She climbed inside as her friends were catching up to her. No one said a word to Brian as they joined Ellen inside the limo.

"What a night," Tanya said.

"A colossal disappointment in every way imaginable," Rich Falcon said.

Ellen couldn't have said it any better herself.

# CHAPTER SIXTEEN

# Back to Montana

B ecause their train wouldn't leave until lunch time, Ellen, Sue, and Tanya invited Rich Falcon to join them in visiting the LaLaurie Museum after breakfast.

The exhibit began with Ellen's painting of Delphine LaLaurie cradling the devil baby as she handed him over to Marie Laveau on the stoop of Lalaurie Mansion. In the painting, the two formidable women and enemies avoided eye contact with one another as they smiled lovingly at the disfigured child. The love that they felt for the misfortunate baby was the only thing they had in common aside from the city where they lived.

Beneath Ellen's painting was a placard with the following message:

*The stories you may have heard about Madame Delphine Lalaurie, her husband, Dr. Louis Lalaurie, and the catastrophic fire that burned the original house in 1834, may or may not hold up to the facts presented to you today in historical documents recently unearthed.*

The sconces on the walls lit the displays of copies made from Dr. Louis LaLaurie's medical journals, Jeanne Blanque's letters, and Delphine's diary. Translations to English were printed in a symmetrical display beside each copy. They were arranged to tell a story, beginning with Delphine's first marriage to Don Ramon when she had just turned thirteen years of age.

"You did this?" Rich Falcon asked Ellen of the painting.

"She did," Tanya said.

"But we all had a hand in discovering the truth about what has been called the Demon Baby of Bourbon Street," Ellen said. "This museum is our tribute to that truth and to the other victims that suffered in the La-Laurie Mansion."

"I think I finally understand the three of you," Rich said. "I didn't understand why you were sticking your noses in tribal affairs, but I get it now. You follow injustices and bring them to light."

Ellen wanted to hug Rich Falcon, but she didn't want to embarrass him. It seemed so infrequent that anyone understood her that it was refreshing when someone did.

They walked through the exhibit together. Ellen was reminded of how proud Paul had been of her and how happy they had been together in the wake of the museum's grand opening. They had resolved to begin a new life together, a plan that had been cut short by Paul's death.

Tears pooled in Ellen's eyes and dripped down her cheeks as they left the museum to head for the train.

An hour into their train ride, Ellen received a phone call from Father Gonzales.

"Hello, Father," she said after she'd put the phone on speaker, so her friends could hear what he had to say. "Our mission was an absolute failure. Please tell me you have better news."

"The buffalo fur had no effect on Sidney Longfellow?" he asked.

"The only effect it had on him was to make him angry," Sue said from across the aisle from Ellen.

"I'm sorry to hear that," the priest said. "Fortunately, I do have some good news."

Ellen and her friends exchanged looks of surprise.

"Don't keep us waiting," Sue said.

"I received a call from Officer Jackson this afternoon. It seems that, of his own volition, Chief Eric Old Person of the Blackfeet Nation provided the forensic team with a sample of his DNA, and they discovered a 25% match with the DNA found on the second of the two bodies, the one previously deemed a John Doe."

"What does that mean?" Ellen asked. "Does that mean Eric Old Person is related to Rabbit?"

"It proves without a doubt that the remains belonged to a Black-foot," the priest explained. "A previous test had confirmed that the body was of Native American descent, but the match with the tribal chief of Blackfeet Nation means that the Blackfeet can claim the body and bury the remains as the tribe sees fit."

"That is wonderful news!" Ellen cried.

"So, the ME still won't say it's Rabbit," Rich Falcon said. "But he will at least say it's a Blackfoot."

"That's correct," Father Gonzales said.

"Thank you," Rich Falcon said with tears in his eyes. "That's good to hear. Rabbit Talks to Buffalo can finally come home, where he belongs. There are so many others, you know—so many other children who were taken from their families who died and were lost to us forever. It's a beautiful thing anytime one who was lost can finally come home."

"If the Blackfeet will allow it," Father Gonzales began, "it's my wish to have Alma Marcello buried in the same casket as Rabbit. They belong together. Don't you agree?"

"I do," Rich Falcon said. "The tribal council must discuss it, but I have a feeling every single one of them will embrace the idea. Thank you, Father Gonzales."

Ellen hoped the burial would be enough. She hoped and prayed that her failure to get Sidney Longfellow to accept the white buffalo fur wouldn't prevent Rabbit from moving on.

Later that night on the train, when Ellen had read as much on her kindle as she could without yawning, she noticed Tanya in the seat beside her wiping away tears.

"Tanya? Are you okay?"

"Yes. I'm sorry."

"Don't apologize. What's wrong?"

"Oh, it's Tina and Johnny's mother. I text her every few days just to check up on the kids, and she rarely responds. I feel like I'm pestering her, but I'm trying to be there for her during a difficult time. I wish she'd let me help her—if not for her sake, for the sake of her kids."

Tanya began to sob.

Ellen put an arm around her. "You just let it out, girlfriend."

Tanya wiped her tears with the backs of her hands. Her bright blue eyes were ringed with red. "I keep thinking about Crow Woman waiting all those years, just in case her son would need her someday. Sometimes I feel that way, too—for my own kids, and now for Tina and Johnny."

"I wonder if all mothers feel that way at one time or another," Ellen said, though it was hard for her to imagine her own mother feeling that way.

"Maybe. I'm sorry. Ignore me. I know you're tired and want to go to sleep."

"Please stop apologizing. You and Sue are my dearest friends. I hope you know how much I love you."

Tanya nodded. "I do, Ellen. And I love you, too."

Sue leaned over the aisle. "I knew you two were closet lesbians. Good for you for finally coming out."

Ellen and Tanya laughed.

"Oh, Sue," Tanya said.

On the second day of the train ride, they had just left Union Station in Chicago, when Ellen received a call from Brian. She hadn't been awake for very long and was in desperate need of caffeine and was afraid her brain was mush, but she took the call.

"Hello," she said.

"I just read your letter," Brian said.

She got up from her seat and made her way to the sightseer lounge, where she wouldn't be overheard by her friends. "I told you to rip it up."

"You know I couldn't do that. Why didn't you tell me, there at the ball?"

"While you were with your date?" Ellen glanced around the lounge, glad there were only a few other passengers visiting with one another and not paying attention to her.

"While we were alone. You could have told me."

"Did you sleep with her?" she asked. She held her breath.

"No, not after I saw you. I couldn't."

"But you slept with her before?"

"You broke things off with me."

"*You* broke things off," she reminded him.

"Only after you'd made it clear that you didn't want me, that you didn't love me as much as I love you," he said.

"I haven't slept with anyone else but you since the day we met," she said.

"Look, Ellen. You distract yourself by renovating historical properties, solving mysteries, and saving ghosts. I distract myself by renovating historical properties and having meaningless sex with women I don't care about. I'm sorry. Okay? But if you're ready to commit to me, if you let me into your heart, even just a little, I'd never sleep with another woman for as long as I lived."

The thought of him loving on that young, beautiful girl sent a shiver of jealousy down her spine.

"I don't know, Brian. I'm scared."

"*You're* scared? *I'm* the one who's scared. *You know* that I'm a sure thing. You've got me wrapped around your finger. But *I*…damn, Ellen. You held back on me. And when you held back, I felt lonely and vulnerable. Can't you understand that?"

She wiped the tears from her eyes. "I'm sorry. I'm so sorry."

"Tell me why you're sorry. Are you sorry because it's not going to work for us? Or are you sorry that you held back on me when you didn't want to?"

"The second, I think."

She heard Brian heave a heavy sigh. "That's a relief."

Ellen wasn't sure what to say next.

"Can I come and see you?" he asked. "Where are you?"

"I'm on a train headed back to Montana."

"Can I come to Montana?"

The thought of seeing him did lift her spirits, but the timing was off. "I want to see you. Really I do."

"But?"

"I came here with Sue and Tanya, to spend time with them. And there's so much going on, so much craziness. You wouldn't believe it."

"Will you tell me about it?" he asked. "I'm especially curious to know why you were in New Orleans and why you were dancing with Sidney Longfellow."

"You know him?"

"He's an acquaintance of mine. I've known him for years."

Ellen sat back in the chair and told Brian the story of Crow Woman and Talks to Buffalo, of her dream with the white buffalo after the hide shocked her, of Rabbit and Sister Alma, of falling into the river, of discovering the bodies, and of the DNA match with Sidney Longfellow.

"Sidney thinks it's a gimmick, but it's all true, Brian."

"Let me give him a call and see what I can do," Brian said.

"He's pretty angry about it and closed-minded, but I suppose it wouldn't hurt to try."

"I'll call you tomorrow and let you know how I make out."

"Thank you, Brian."

"My pleasure, Ellen. Goodbye."

"Goodbye."

Ellen and her friends arrived at Glacier Park Lodge on Sunday night. They got Rich Falcon a cab ride home and walked across the parking lot and headed to their room—to the one room they'd kept for the week. They had chosen Sue's room because it was a suite with a king-size bed and a pull-out sofa. Sue insisted that Ellen and Tanya take the bed, saying that she didn't want her snoring to keep them up all night. Ellen and Tanya were too tired to argue. Everyone changed into their night clothes, brushed their teeth, and crashed.

CHAPTER SEVENTEEN

# Sidney Longfellow

E llen, wake up," Tanya said from across the king-size bed.
Ellen glanced at the digital clock on the nightstand. It was
only eight o'clock in the morning.

"Please, Tanya, let me sleep. Go to breakfast without me."

"It's not that. Your phone keeps ringing. You must not have turned
the ringer off last night when we got back. Will you please make it stop?
I want to sleep, too."

"Oh. I'm sorry."

Mortified that it had been disturbing her friend, Ellen searched for
her phone. It wasn't on the nightstand. She felt beneath her pillow and
came up empty. She climbed out of bed and checked the floor. Then
she heard it ringing in her purse.

She stumbled across the room and fished it out. She didn't recognize
the number.

"Hello?" she said into the phone.

"Hello, Mrs. Mohr. This is Eric Old Person."

"Oh, hello." She had no idea why the chief of the Blackfeet would be
calling her, especially at this hour. A glance at her phone revealed that
she had four missed calls from him already. "How are you? Is everything
okay?"

"Everything is more than okay. I am calling you to personally invite
you and your two companions to the burial ceremony of Rabbit Talks to

Buffalo and Alma Marcello this Thursday the 29th at Talks to Buffalo Lodge after sunset."

"Thank you, Chief Old Person. We'd be happy to attend."

"I wanted to call you as soon as possible to let you know that Sidney Longfellow has reached out to me and has asked to be included in the burial ceremony of his grandfather."

Ellen almost dropped the phone. "What? He has? Oh, my goodness!"

"For this reason, many of us will be fasting this week. We will participate in purification ceremonies and vision quests so that we can be more open to the spirit guides as we forge this new relationship with Mr. Longfellow and as we help Crow Woman and Rabbit to find their way to our ancestral grounds."

"Oh, I see."

"I wanted to call you as early as possible this morning so that you and your companions could begin your fasting, too, so you can join us tonight for purification and prayer at the Two-Badger Medicine."

"Tonight?"

"Yes. You said you wanted a vision quest, didn't you, Mrs. Mohr?"

"I did. I do. Are you saying that's happening tonight?"

"It begins tonight and will last four days," he said. "After that, we will break our fast together with prayer and preparation of the ground for the return of our loved ones to the earth."

Ellen thanked the chief again for his invitation. Then she raised her hands in the air and danced around the room with glee, careful not to disturb her snoring roommates.

An hour later, after she'd showered and dressed and Tanya and Sue had finally begun to stir, Ellen told them about her conversation with Eric Old Person.

"What a shocker!" Sue said.

Tanya stifled a yawn. "I wonder what changed Sidney's mind."

"I think it was Brian," Ellen said.

Sue pouted her lips. "Does this mean we aren't having breakfast this morning? I was so looking forward to eating something other than train food."

"It really wasn't very good, was it," Tanya agreed.

"No," Sue said. "And it seems hardly fair that the garbage we ate on the train will be our last meal before four days of fasting. I've never gone that long without food, I don't think. Have you?"

"I don't think so," Tanya said. "And I'm not sure I *can* go that long."

"Then are we agreed that we should wait to begin our fast after a big breakfast?" Sue asked. "That's what we did before our last purification ceremony, and no one was the wiser for it."

"But Eric Old Person went to so much trouble to call us early this morning," Ellen said. "Won't we feel guilty?"

"Nope," Sue said. "You, Tanya?"

"Not at all."

Ellen gave them a sheepish grin. "Then I guess I'm outvoted."


Ellen and her friends were just finishing up their gorging on eggs, bacon, waffles, and hash brown potatoes in the Glacier Park Lodge Restaurant overlooking the pristine mountain views when Ellen's phone rang again from another number she did not recognize.

"Hello?" she said into her phone.

"Hello, Ellen, this is Sidney Longfellow."

Ellen's heart seemed to skip a beat, and she found it hard to find her tongue.

"I hope you don't mind me calling you. I got your number from Brian."

"Um, no, Sidney. I don't mind at all."

Sue and Tanya's brows shot up. Sue mouthed, "Put him on speaker!"

Ellen quickly did the phone on speaker just as Sidney said, "Good. I wanted to apologize to you and to your friends for the way I behaved."

Tanya's jaw dropped open.

"That's not necessary," Ellen said. "We sprang something life-altering on you from out of the blue. Your disbelief was to be expected."

"Thank you for that."

Ellen said, "Chief Eric Old Person called me earlier this morning. I was shocked by the news. What changed your mind?"

"I'd like to talk to you about that in person. My wife and I should be arriving at Glacier Park Lodge this afternoon. Would you and your friends care to join us in the lobby around two o'clock?"

Now *Sue's* jaw dropped open. Ellen raised her brows as if to say, *Can we meet him at two?*

Sue and Tanya nodded.

"Two o'clock would be fine," Ellen said.

"Then it's a date. I'll see you then."

The call ended.

Ellen and her friends were speechless.


"What time are we supposed to be at the Badger-Two Medicine tonight for the purification ceremony and vision quest?" Sue asked as she, Ellen, and Tanya left their room in the Glacier Park Lodge and headed for the elevator.

"Five o'clock," Tanya said.

Sue pushed the down button when they reached the elevators. "Then don't you think we could eat one more time?"

"I feel like I'm going to faint," Tanya admitted.

"It's only been five hours," Ellen pointed out as the elevator doors opened. "How will we last four days if we can't even make it for five hours?"

As they climbed into the elevator, Sue said, "We might have a better chance of making it four days if we eat one more time."

Ellen shook her head. "You do what you want. I already feel bad enough for having breakfast."

"Well, you're no fun," Sue said.

Sidney Longfellow was already in the lobby seated on a rustic sofa beside a lovely woman in her seventies whom Ellen recognized from his family photos as his wife. The two of them stood up as Ellen and her friends approached them.

Sidney was wearing a crisp white shirt without a tie with the top button undone beneath a gray dinner jacket. With that he wore crisp denim jeans and gray leather cowboy boots. His wife, who looked just like her photos in his office, with her curly blonde shoulder-length hair, blue eyes, and pink cheeks, was wearing a pink rayon pantsuit and taupe pumps. She also wore a short strand of pearls around her neck and several rings on her fingers. Ellen was beginning to feel underdressed and frumpy in her cotton blouse, capri pants, and loafers.

Sidney offered each of them his hand. "It's good to see you again. This is my wife, Sheila Ann."

"It's nice to meet you," they said to her.

"Likewise," Sheila Ann said as she, too, shook each of their hands.

"Please have a seat," Sidney said, motioning to the sofa facing the one where he and his wife had been sitting.

Ellen and Tanya sat on either side of Sue.

"I want to apologize again for my rude behavior in New Orleans," Sidney said as he took his seat beside his wife.

"We understand," Sue said. "But we're curious to hear what changed your mind."

"Well, it wasn't any one thing," Sidney said. "It started with that white buffalo fur. When I bumped into it at the dance, it felt almost like I'd touched a live wire."

Ellen lifted her brows and glanced at her friends. "Then you *are* the rightful owner."

"I'm afraid I don't know what that means," he said.

"The Blackfeet believe that the Creator chooses who can and can't kill the rare white buffalo," Ellen explained. "The person who kills the buffalo cannot sell the hide. The hide belongs to him until he passes it on to a relative after he dies. Rabbit—that is, your grandfather—was unable to receive the hide from his father or to pass it on to his son. Since you are the only living son of his son, it belongs to you."

"I see," Sidney said.

"I shouldn't have interrupted," Ellen said. "Please finish what you were saying."

"All right, then," Sidney said. "Well, I still didn't think much of your story, even after that strange feeling at the benefit. But then Brian McManius called me yesterday morning and told me all about you three ladies—how you found his missing brother when no one, not even the FBI, could help him."

The memories of her time in Portland swept over Ellen, reminding her of the days when she'd first began to fall for Brian. She felt her cheeks grow warm.

"Then he told me what you've been up to here in Montana," he said.

"I find it very fascinating," Sheila Ann said. "Especially the part about the rods pulling you from a boat and into the river where Sidney's grandfather lay!"

"Look at you getting all the credit," Sue teased Ellen.

Sidney said, "Brian convinced me that it wouldn't hurt to check out your story by simply looking at my parents' birth certificates. Imagine my surprise when I discovered that my father had no birth certificate. Instead, there were adoption records. He'd been adopted from the Ursuline nuns."

Ellen scooted to the edge of the couch and leaned forward with her elbows on her knees. "But that didn't prove that you are descended from the Blackfeet."

"No," he said.

Sheila Ann also leaned forward. "But we'd just been told your story—about Sister Alma and Rabbit."

Sidney patted his wife's hand. "I called the convent and asked them to look into my father's records. The mother superior didn't know anything about it. They aren't an orphanage, you see. They don't normally take in unwanted infants and adopt them out. But she did some digging, and she found the admission records from 1909 confirming that an Ursuline nun returned from Holy Family Mission with an orphaned baby boy."

"That cemented it for us," Sheila Ann said.

"Well, what cemented it for me was a dream I had while napping yesterday afternoon—at least, I think it was a dream. I didn't know I'd fallen asleep."

"He dreamed of the white buffalo," Sheila Ann explained.

Ellen glanced excitedly at her friends.

"Did the white buffalo speak to you?" Sue asked.

"He did. He said he was glad to finally meet me." Sidney Longfellow wiped a tear from his eye.

# CHAPTER EIGHTEEN

# The Vision Quest

M onday evening, the shuttle dropped Ellen, Sue, Tanya, and the Longfellows near the thick pines surrounding the Badger-Two Medicine. As they'd been instructed to do, they carried nothing with them, not even their phones. Waiting for them on the side of the road were Rich Falcon and Karen Murray. They had blankets and skins draped across their shoulders and backs. They handed skins and blankets to Ellen and each member of her party. Ellen was glad to wrap herself in them, for the evening air was cold.

After introductions were made between the Blackfeet and the Longfellows, Karen led their party down the hill to the valley below as she explained about collecting the materials for their sweat lodge. Ellen noticed four other groups of six to eight people also building sweat lodges near the Missouri River. She recognized many of the people from the Sun Dance that had taken place two weeks before. Chief Eric Old Person, Jack Stone, and Terry Murray were among them.

Once the willow branches had been chosen and cleaned of leaves, Karen and Rich built the frame while the others spread the sage and collected the rocks. Then Rich built a fire while Karen helped them to cover the frame with the blankets and hides.

Carrying a pipe and a canteen and wearing a colorful robe across her shoulders, Karen climbed into the newly built sweat lodge and sat facing the door. Rich held open the flap so the others could climb inside and have a seat. As before, they sat crossed legged in a circle with their knees touching. Rich completed the circle near the door and closed the flap, covering them with darkness.

A rustling sound was soon followed by the strike of a match. The light of the match illuminated Karen's face as she lit her pipe on one end and sucked air from the other. In the small circle of light, Karen's face appeared transformed. She no longer looked like Karen the provost of the community college or Karen the public relations representative of the tribe or Karen the tribal secretary; she looked like Karen the medicine woman, and she looked like a bad ass.

In the next moment, Karen blew out the match, and her face disappeared in the darkness.

"The purpose of this purification ceremony is to prepare our bodies to receive messages from our spirit guides," Karen said. "We fast and suffer the challenges of the elements for four days and four nights to make our bodies worthy and open. Before we begin with the first round, please state why you are here seeking a vision. I'll begin."

Ellen heard Karen draw from the pipe. As she exhaled, she said, "I seek a vision that will help me to protect this sacred land, home of my ancestors, from being violated or tainted by modern technology."

The pipe was suddenly thrust into Ellen's lap. She put the end of it to her lips and sucked in the smoke. Slowly she exhaled. "I seek a vision that will show me how to help Rabbit and Crow Woman to find peace. I also seek guidance in finding my own personal peace."

Sue and Tanya echoed Ellen's words, and Rich Falcon echoed Karen's.

When it was Sidney's turn to speak, he said, "I seek a vision that will help me to better understand my Indian heritage."

Sheila Ann took the pipe and drew from it. Then, in a shaky voice, she said, "I need guidance in how to carry on."

Ellen heard sniffles in the darkness, and when Rich Falcon opened the flap to place coals in the center of the lodge, Ellen caught a glimpse of the other faces. It was a quick glimpse, for when Karen poured the medicine water onto the coals, Rich dropped the flap, and the coals sizzled as steam filled the room. But it had been enough of a glimpse to see that Sidney and Sheila Ann were weeping.

Karen said. "Now we pray for thanks."

Karen and Rich began to sing a song in their native tongue as the pipe was passed around a second time. Rich added more coals. Karen doused them with medicine water. The steam thickened. And more prayers were sung. Then Karen began to chant the four beats of crow and four beats of wolf that Ellen recalled from her last purification ceremony. Ellen and the others joined the chanting.

Ellen could feel the effects of the medicine in the pipe and the steam. Her neck and shoulders relaxed. She felt mellow, almost sleepy. She closed her eyes and opened her heart to the spirits.

The pipe had gone around five times when Karen stopped chanting. The others followed suit.

"Let me tell you what to expect on your vision quest," Karen said. "I will give you each a small pipe with some tobacco, sweet grass, and sage. Then I will lead you across the river and up the mountain, where you should go off on your own to await your vision."

Sue cleared her throat. "Are we really expected to go without food and water for four whole days?"

"If you can't make it," Rich began, "you can always return to the camp. We have food and water here and helpers, who will be praying for us."

"But push yourself," Karen said. "We deprive ourselves of food and water so that our bodies are more like the spirits. It makes it easier for us to see them and to hear them."

"And if you get your vision before the fourth day," Rich said, "you can come down early, break your fast, and pray with the helpers."

"But if you don't," Karen said, "listen for the conch. At the end of the fourth day, one of the helpers here at the camp will blow a conch, just before sunset. When you hear that, then you'll know that it's time to return from the mountain."

"Then we'll break our fast and caravan over to Talks to Buffalo Lodge for the burial ceremony," Rich said.

"And we'll begin the burial ceremony by sharing our visions with the community," Karen said.

Outside the tent, a drum began to beat a quick, steady rhythm.

"Before we join the others for the trek up the mountain," Karen said, "I will pray over you. I pray for your strength to endure the trials of this journey, and I pray for the willingness of the spirits to give us their messages."

Karen then said a string of syllables in her native language. When she'd finished, Rich Falcon opened the flap to the door of the lodge and stepped outside. Then he helped the others to do the same.

The sun had already set, and darkness covered the Two-Badger Medicine, but the light from the emerging stars above, along with a nearly full moon, offered enough light to see by. A chill in the air made Ellen shiver as she wrapped her cable-knit cardigan more tightly around her. She envied the tribal members in their thick jackets and robes.

She now saw the helpers sitting on blankets near their sweat lodges with their campfires. They were singing to the beat of the drum as the other groups marched toward the river.

Rich gave each of the questers in their group a small pipe already filled with dried herbs, a pillar candle standing about six inches tall and three inches in diameter, and a matchbook.

"No water, flashlight, or first aid kit, I suppose?" Sue asked playfully.

"Sorry," Rich said.

"I hope we won't regret this," Ellen whispered to Sidney and Sheila Ann.

"I find it rather exciting," Sheila Ann replied. "I just hope I'm capable of making the journey. These old legs aren't what they used to be."

Karen, who had overheard, said, "You don't have to do this, if you don't feel you can. You can remain here and pray for the others."

"I want to go," Sheila Ann said.

"The helpers will be keeping an eye out for us," Rich explained. "They'll be able to see us on the mountainside from the camp. If you get into trouble, just wave a match, and someone will come to help you."

"That's good to know," Tanya said.

Karen led their group behind the other questers, who were already hiking through a shallow part of the river. Ellen and Tanya followed Karen. Sue and Sheila Ann went at a slower pace. Rich and Sidney helped them along. Fortunately, they were the last group, so they weren't holding anyone up.

"There's no bridge?" Tanya asked Rich when they reached the river.

"There's nothing here that wasn't already here ten thousand years ago," he said.

Sue scoffed. "I doubt these trees are that old."

"No, but they look exactly like the trees that our people looked upon in the very beginning."

"Or so you think," Sue argued. "Since you weren't here to see it for yourself."

Rich laughed. "Or so we believe. Yes."

Ellen followed Karen into the river. The water, which reached their shins, was freezing cold.

"Geez Louise!" Ellen cried.

"What have you and Sue gotten me into?" Tanya complained beside her.

"Wait up, you two," Sue said. "I hear you talking about me."

"Oh, dear!" Sheila Ann squealed. "I wasn't expecting it to be this cold in July!"

"Speak up if you want to turn back," Karen said from the front of their line.

Tanya said, "I wonder how long it will take our pants and shoes and socks to dry."

"They may not dry completely," Rich said, "but it's part of the suffering we endure to prepare ourselves to receive the vision."

Ellen glanced back at her friends, who were frowning.

Once they'd crossed the river, Karen said, "From here on out, please refrain from talking, unless it's an emergency. If you listen carefully, you will hear the others singing one of our traditional songs. You can hum along, if you'd like, or you can pray silently as we hike up the mountain."

The mountainside was steep. Ellen found herself huffing and puffing in no time at all. She prayed for the strength to endure, and she prayed for the strength of the others, too.

Despite the cool night, sweat formed on Ellen's face and neck. They hiked for what felt like an hour before the drumming stopped. Karen turned to Ellen and the others and told them to find a place to sit or lie down to smoke and pray alone.

Ellen hugged her friends for luck. Sue looked like she was going to pass out but said nothing before they went their separate ways, disappearing among the pines and cypress trees.

There were no trails as Ellen picked her way through the woods, searching for a spot. She didn't want to go too far, afraid that she wouldn't be able to find her way back. The songs of the helpers below reassured her as she found a flat rocky spot and sat down.

First, she lit her candle. Then she lit her pipe. She gazed up at the bright stars overhead and asked the spirits to speak. As if in answer, a lone wolf howled across the mountainside. Ellen wondered if it came from an actual wolf, or if the sound had been made by one of the Indians.

If someone had asked her five years ago, before she bought the Gold House, if she would ever go on a vision quest to commune with spirits in the mountains, she would have laughed. It was interesting to compare the woman she was then to the woman she was now, even if the woman she was now wasn't fully formed.

She lay back on the flat rock and closed her eyes. She was so tired and cold and hungry. At some point, she fell asleep.

She was awakened when something cold pressed against her neck. At first, she thought it was a small dog—a long-haired Dachshund. Brown round eyes seemed to smile up at her. But when she reached out to pet him, saying, "Well, hello, there," she realized it wasn't a dog but a little red fox.

Instantly, she thought of Crow Woman and Cute Fox. Could this animal, who felt as real as she did, be a spirit animal? And, if so, could it possibly be Cute Fox?

"Nolan is trying to reach you," the fox said. "He has important news."

The fox licked her cheek and ran away.

Ellen lay back, stunned. She stared at the bright stars and the nearly full moon overhead, wondering how long she had been asleep before awakened by the fox. It occurred to her that she might still be asleep. She pinched herself.

Then, the white buffalo, tall and luminous and stately, walked up beside her and gazed down at her. The stars twinkled behind him, and the bright moon made a halo of light around his horns.

"Am I dreaming?" she asked. "Or am I awake?"

"What's the difference?" he said.

Ellen thought about his answer as the buffalo walked away.

"Wait!" she called to him as she sat up. "Where are you going?"

"To talk to my grandson," he said. "Thanks to you."

She watched him, transfixed by his grace and luminous glow, as he disappeared in the trees.

At that moment, she saw something in the tree nearest her. It was a large bird—a great horned owl. He had huge yellow eyes and two tufts of feathers set high on his head, resembling horns. His feathers were brown, with dark brown spots, except for those at his throat, which were white.

She'd seen him before.

He said, "You awake? Me tooooo. You awake? Me tooooo."

"Did you come here all the way from Boulder City?" she wondered out loud.

The owl shook his head from side to side.

"I follow youuuu," he said. "I follow youuuuu."

"Ellen?"

Ellen turned toward the sound of her name to find Paul standing a few feet away in the light of the moon. He wore the suit he'd been buried in. His blue eyes glistened beneath the stars and his peach lips parted into a grin,

He looked so much like his old self that, for a moment, she wondered if his death, and all that had happened after, had been a dream. Maybe she was just waking up from a very strange dream and Paul was here to take her home.

"Are you alive?" she finally asked.

"My spirit is," he said.

Disappointment washed over her. "Oh." Then she asked, "Haven't you moved on? Aren't you at peace?"

"Yes, Ellen. I am at peace. But I need you to find peace, too."

Her stomach clenched into a knot as she wondered if she, too, had passed from the world of the living. "Am I dead?"

"Not physically," he said. "But your spirit is languid and needs a reboot. Isn't that why you're here?"

"I suppose so," she said. "Why are *you* here?"

"To tell you that's it okay to go on without me. I sent a message to you last year. Remember Edna?"

Tears filled her eyes. "Even if you aren't real, even if this is only a dream, I'm so happy to see you."

He took a few steps toward her. She climbed to her feet. They stood facing one another, inches apart. Then he put his arms around her and kissed her cheek—and she felt it! She felt his strong arms and the touch of his lips against her skin. He felt as real as if he were alive!

"Oh, Paul!" she cried.

She was startled by the sound of a horn. She looked down the mountainside, searching for signs of the helpers below but found only darkness. And yet the horn blew. She turned back to Paul and gasped. He was gone.

Her stomach dropped.

"Paul? Paul, please come back!"

A twig snapped nearby. Ellen turned to see Karen. Her face glowed in the light of the flame flickering on the end of her candle.

"It's time to go," Karen said.

"Aren't we staying for four days?" Ellen asked.

"It's been four days. Come on. Grab your things and follow me."

CHAPTER NINETEEN

# The Burial Ceremony

As Ellen followed Karen Murray down the mountainside, she wondered what had become of her friends, especially when she caught up to Sidney Longfellow, who said, "Have you seen Sheila Ann?"

"No," Ellen said. "Have you seen Tanya or Sue?"

Sidney shook his head.

Karen led them across the shallow part of the freezing river and back to camp, where Sue and Tanya were siting with Sheila Ann and Rich Falcon on blankets around a campfire.

"What are you eating?" Ellen asked them as chills crept up her body from her drenched legs and feet.

"Come and have some," Rich Falcon said.

She sat beside Rich on the blanket and moved her feet close to the fire. He handed her a cup of nuts and berries. She poured some into her mouth.

"It's actually quite tasty, isn't it," Sue said without inflection. "But maybe anything tastes good—even tree bark—after four days of nothing."

"Did you have a good quest?" Ellen asked her.

"I saw my mother," Sue said. "It was kind of crazy, actually. I was just telling the others that she was trying to teach me the Rumba, of all things. She said it would be important for my future."

Their little group around the fire busted out laughing—all except Karen Murray, who said, "I can tell you what it means, Sue. Your mother is letting you know that she will always be there for you, no matter how crazy your life gets."

Sue brushed a tear from her cheek and said, "I guess I can't get rid of her that easily, huh?"

Karen smiled. "I guess not."

"What about you, Ellen?" Tanya asked. "You were up there for a long time. Did you have a good quest?"

"It went by fast," Ellen said. "I was visited by a fox, a white buffalo, a horned owl, and, best of all, Paul."

"What an honor!" Rich said. "To be visited by so many spirit guides during one vision quest is rare."

"That's true," Karen said. "You might just have the makings of a medicine woman. Do you have Indian blood in your family?"

Ellen bit her lip. "My grandmother used to say she had Cherokee ancestors, but I was never told anything more about it."

"Interesting," Karen said.

Ellen turned to Tanya. "What about you? Did you have a good quest"

"I saw my parents. They came to me as cardinals."

"Really? How cool! What did they say?" Ellen asked.

"That I was brave," Tanya said laughing. "What a joke, right?"

"But you are brave," Karen said. "Look where you are. It takes bravery to be here."

After they'd eaten their snack and had their fill of water, the questers and helpers gathered up their things and walked up the hill from Two-Badger Medicine toward the road, where a dozen vehicles were parked. Sidney and his wife were offered a ride in a van with the chief, Terry Murray, and Jack Stone. Ellen and her friends rode with Karen in her black Honda Accord. Rich drove another group in his van. The caravan made its way down the dark road toward the reservation and Talks to Buffalo Lodge.

Ellen was surprised by how many cars were already parked in front of the dilapidated house near the old Chevy pickup with no wheels. A string of lights behind the house illuminated the path as Ellen followed the others past the rotting fence to one of the dead trees in back where a table had been laid out with turkey legs, cobs of corn, and watermelon slices. Others were already eating as they sat on blankets on the ground. They used no utensils or plates and ate only what they could carry with two hands.

"When in Rome," Sue said as she picked up a turkey leg and a cob of corn.

Ellen and Tanya laughed, and after choosing a cob and a turkey leg of their own, followed Sue to find a spot to eat. That's when they saw Father Gonzales waving to them from where he was sitting on a blanket with a fellow priest. The ladies carried their food through the crowd to say hello.

"Father O'Brien, these are the ladies I told you about," Father Gonzales said before introducing them.

Father O'Brien was older and rounder than his companion. He wore round spectacles beneath bushy white brows.

"Please have a seat," Father O'Brien said. "We were beginning to feel a bit ostracized. No one wanted to sit with us."

"I'm so grateful that this day has finally arrived," Father Gonzales said.

Ellen, Sue, and Tanya told the Jesuit priests about their vision quests as they ate their meal. As they listened, Father O'Brien said very little, but Father Gonzales was fascinated and full of questions. Ellen and her friends hadn't finished answering his questions when Chief Eric Old Person walked to the front of the crowd and asked everyone to pray with him.

The chief spoke in his own language for several minutes. Ellen noticed him pointing to the casket beside him. It was sitting on the ground beside a deep hole beneath the dead tree.

In English, the chief said, "We pray for the spirits of Crow Woman and Rabbit. We also pray for Rabbit's wife, Alma Marcello. For the first time, we welcome Rabbit back to his home, back to his people. We pray that he and his mother and wife may finally let go of the pain they experienced while alive so that they can dwell peacefully among our ancestors, including Talks to Buffalo, who waits for them there."

The chief paused for a moment of silence before saying, "And now we will hear from a few of the questers. Who would like to speak first?"

To Ellen's astonishment, Sidney Longfellow stood up. "I have something to say."

Everyone was silent as Sidney made his way to the front of the group beside the chief and the casket beneath the old tree.

"When I was a young man, I felt a strong attraction to this land," he said. "Back then, in my early thirties, I didn't know about my Blackfeet ancestors. My brother, may he rest in peace, and I were petroleum engineers driven by a desire to make a difference in the world. We hoped to help our nation, the United States of America, become independent from foreign oil. So, when Ronald Reagan decided to offer gas and oil leases in the Badger-Two Medicine in the early eighties, I took that as a sign. You see, it married the inexplicable attraction I felt to this area with my desire to provide domestic gas and oil to my country."

The crowd was so quiet, that Ellen could hear her own heart beating.

"Up until recently, I couldn't fathom why the Blackfeet had any right to get in the way of my dream. From my point of view, they didn't own the land, and the government had granted me legal rights. For forty years, my hands were tied. I watched my dream come to nothing as I went from being an idealistic young man to a disillusioned old one."

Ellen heard sniffling. She looked across the yard to see Sheila Ann sitting on the edge of a blanket beside Rich Falcon with her face in her hands.

"My days are numbered," Sidney said. "I realize that all our days are numbered, but you see, I have stage four cancer. I won't be here much longer—at least, not in this old body. I can't tell you how grateful I am for the chance to discover ancestors I didn't know I had, for a chance to learn about a heritage I didn't know was mine."

Sidney wiped tears from his eyes and cleared his throat. "During my vision quest, my grandfather, Rabbit Talks to Buffalo, appeared to me as a white buffalo. He had already visited me in a dream, but this time, I was awake when I saw him. He told me that he was sorry for the struggle I'd endured with the gas and oil lease but that it was the ancestors' way of bringing me back to them."

Sidney's voice cracked on those final words. When he could speak again, he said, "I promise you, my brother and sisters, that the first thing I will do tomorrow morning will be to call my attorney and order him to halt all legal proceedings related to rights to drill on the Badger-Two Medicine!"

The crowd erupted with applause and cheers. People jumped to their feet and embraced one another. Others shouted with joy. Many of the people openly wept tears of relief.

Ellen noticed Rich Falcon enter the back of the house and return with the white buffalo hide, which glowed, luminous, in the moonlight. With tears streaming down his cheeks, Rich maneuvered with the hide through the crowd and placed it on the shoulders of Sidney Longfellow.

Sidney accepted the robe with a handshake. Then he wiped his eyes and returned to Sheila Ann. He took her into his arms, and the two of them wept together.

After the cheering and the singing and dancing had died down, six more of the questers stood up to talk about their visions, the last of which was Karen Murray.

"Crow Woman came to me," Karen said.

Ellen gasped and covered her mouth as she glanced at Sue and Tanya.

"She came to me as a great crow and said in the language of our people, 'I am Crow Woman, wife of Talks to Buffalo, and mother of Rabbit. I cannot and will not forgive what the U.S. government did to my son and to our people. For years, I tried to destroy the sons of those who dared to live in the house where my Rabbit was taken away. Now, I am grateful that my son has come home, and I am thankful to those who made it happen. I cannot and will not forgive the injustice committed against me and our people, but those responsible have already died. It is up to the living to rectify past wrongs. Because my son has been found, I will move on.'"

Karen and the other questers who had spoken returned to their seats. The chief prayed over the casket as it was interred. Father Gonzales said a few words about Alma. Then the chief led the Blackfeet in a final prayer.

When the ceremony was over, Tanya reached over and put one arm around Sue and the other around Ellen. "What a night," she said, grinning from ear to ear. "I don't suppose it's too late for you guys to let me in on the renovation of Talks to Buffalo Lodge, is it?"

Sue turned to Ellen. "Hmm. What do you think? Should we give her a chance to redeem herself?"

"She did come and rescue us from here," Ellen said. "But I'm not sure."

"You guys!" Tanya said with a mock huff.


It was nearly midnight when Ellen, Sue, and Tanya returned to their room at Glacier Park Lodge. The first thing they did was check their phones. Ellen had a missed call from Brian and another from Nolan. Both had left her a message.

The first was from Brian:

*Hi, Ellen. I know you're away on your vision quest, but I just wanted to call to let you know that I'm thinking of you. Love ya. Bye.*

Ellen smiled gleefully before listening to the message from Nolan:

*Hi, Mom. Will you call me as soon as you can? Everything's fine. I just have something important to tell you.*

Ellen remembered what the red fox had told her on the mountainside. She was tempted to call Nolan right then and there. There was a possibility that he'd be working the night shift at the hospital and would be able to accept her call, but she didn't want to risk waking him and making him groggy for the rest of his day.

As she readied for bed, she wondered what important thing her son wanted to tell her.

CHAPTER TWENTY

# Coming Home

It wasn't until Ellen and her friends were on the train heading back to San Antonio that Ellen finally got a hold of Nolan over the phone.

"Hey, sweet boy," she said. "I'm so sorry we keep missing each other. I'm dying to know what you want to tell me."

"Are you sitting down?" he asked.

"Yes." She bit her lip, wondering what on earth he would say. Had he saved someone's life? Had his residency ended? Was he moving back to San Antonio from Oklahoma?

"I asked Taylor to marry me, and she said yes!"

"What?" Ellen took a second to process what she'd just heard. Then joy coursed through her heart as she glanced over at her friends. "You're engaged?"

"Yes, Mom. Taylor and I are getting married, and we're hoping you'll help us with the wedding."

Ellen laughed out loud and squealed with excitement. Several passengers turned around to look at her.

"My son's getting married!" she said to them.

They turned back around in their seats without so much as a congratulations, but Ellen didn't mind. She was so happy for her son and was thrilled that he wanted her to be a part of this important time in his life.

Once the shock and surprise had worn off, she asked him, "When you say you want my help with the wedding, what does that mean? Because you know I'm happy to pay for it."

"Thanks, Mom. I had a feeling you'd say that. Taylor and I were also hoping you'd help us to plan it. She wants a big wedding but neither of us have any time, and her parents, well, don't repeat this to a soul. Taylor says they have no sense of style."

"She thinks *I* have a sense of style?" Ellen asked. "I love her already and would be more than happy to help in any way I can."

Ellen was tired and exhausted when the train finally pulled into Sunset Station in San Antonio late Wednesday night. It was the first week of August, and the Texas heat was merciless, even after dark. She and her friends found their bags, dismounted the train, and dragged their luggage toward the parking lot, where Dave, Tanya's husband, would be waiting to give them a ride home.

Standing beside Dave and his silver Porsche under the light of a streetlamp was Brian.

As Ellen approached him with her mouth hanging open, he said, "I know you're tired and that this probably wasn't a good idea, but I couldn't wait…"

She didn't give him a chance to finish. She rushed into his arms and pressed her lips to his.

Over the next four months, Ellen, Sue, and Tanya made three different trips to Montana to meet with the contractor they'd chosen to spearhead the renovation of Talks to Buffalo Lodge. Between Nolan's wedding plans and the renovations, Ellen discovered an improved knack for making decisions. She knew what she liked and was able to choose color palettes, fabrics, finishes, décor, and accessories like it was no one's business. Both her friends and her family seemed impressed.

Ellen was overjoyed that both the wedding and the renovations allowed her to spend more time with friends and family. Sue and Tanya threw a bridal shower for Taylor at Sue's house. Alison and Lane hosted a couples' shower for Nolan and Taylor at Ellen's house. One afternoon, Alison joined Ellen, Taylor, and Taylor's mother and sister at the bridal shop, where they searched for just the right wedding gown for the bride. But it was the day that she, Lane, and Alison met Nolan at a tuxedo rental in Austin that Ellen had her big cry. Once they settled on the right choice, seeing her firstborn son wearing the tuxedo he would wear on his wedding day filled Ellen with overwhelming emotion. She wished Paul could be there, too, and hoped he was watching down on Nolan with pride and joy.

In between her trips to Montana and the wedding festivities, Ellen entertained Brian in San Antonio or traveled to Portland to see him. She had taken Paul's words on the mountainside to heart. He'd told her that it was okay for her to move on without him. He'd set her free. She was still struggling with what that meant, but she was making progress.

One evening, she was lying in bed in Brian's arms after a particularly romantic evening with him at her home in San Antonio when, out of the blue, she had a vision of the white buffalo. It approached her side of the bed for a fleeting second and disappeared.

She sat up and turned on the bedside lamp. "Did you see that?"

Brian yawned. "See what?"

Ellen jumped from the bed and looked around the room. She checked the hall and the master bath but saw no sign of her visitor.

"Everything okay?" Brian asked.

"I saw the white buffalo again," she said as she returned to the bed and to his arms. "I wonder why he came to me."

The next day, Brian found her answer. Over breakfast, he showed her a headline in the *New York Times* announcing the death of oil and gas tycoon, Sidney Longfellow.

"Do you think he came to say goodbye?" she asked Brian.

"Well, it couldn't have been a coincidence."

That afternoon after Brian had left, Ellen did two things. She wrote a letter to Sheila Ann, expressing her condolences and reminding her to pass the white buffalo fur to one of her children. Then she went to her studio behind her house and began to paint.

It took her a few days to finish the painting. In the end, she was pleased with how it turned out. She depicted the magnificent, luminous white buffalo as he had appeared to her on the mountainside beneath the starry night in the Two-Badger Medicine. She hoped her friends would agree to allow her to place it on the mantle over the hearth at Talks to Buffalo Lodge.

Nolan and Taylor were married in April the weekend after Easter, when the church was still decorated with Easter flowers. Although Ellen was happy to have Brian standing beside her as she watched her firstborn begin a new chapter in his life, she could sense Paul's presence there, too. In that moment, Ellen realized that she could love Brian fully and completely, knowing that Paul was watching over her and witnessing the important moments in their children's lives. She realized that to move forward, she didn't have to *let go* of the past but to *move on* from it. She could cherish it and cherish Paul while moving forward to a future that included Brian.

The following June, nearly a year after Ellen, Sue, and Tanya had first traveled to East Glacier Park, Montana, the renovations of Talks to Buffalo Lodge were complete. Sue and Tanya and their husbands met Ellen and Brian for a final walk-through with the contractor.

Ellen and her friends had been careful to preserve as much of the original structure as they possibly could without compromising its integrity. For example, they used the good floorboards from the second story to replace the rotten boards downstairs, so the entire first floor was original. Then they refloored the second story with new planks similar in color and style to the old.

Although the roof and ceiling had to be replaced, they sheathed the new beams with wood from the old ones. The stone around the fireplace was also original and was brought to life by the simple use of a power sprayer. Up on the mantle, also made from one of the original beams, was Ellen's painting of the white buffalo. And, in front of the hearth was the restored bench that once held the sacred hide.

The kitchen was the only room that strayed from the theme of historical preservation. Ellen and her friends had agreed that they wanted a modern look with granite countertops and stainless-steel appliances. The cabinets were painted a light gray that brought out the silver veins in the granite.

The three couples stayed in the house over the weekend, drawing straws for the master. Sue tried to avoid the random drawing, arguing that she couldn't go up and down the stairs as easily as the others, but Ellen and Tanya insisted, and Sue won anyway.

Together, the three couples explored Glacier National Park. They revisited some of the places Ellen, Sue, and Tanya had seen on their first trip, and they ventured out to other areas, too. They even hiked to the lake where Rich Falcon had showed them the Grizzly Bears, and they were lucky to see a mother nursing two cubs on the shore.

Weeping Wall was one of the places Ellen was determined to revisit. She stood beside Brian gazing at it from across the street as cars drove through the falling water.

"It's an interesting symbol for both the past and the present, don't you think?" Brian said.

"In what way?" she asked.

"If you think about it, it seems to be lamenting the sins of the past while baptizing the passing cars with renewed life."

Ellen shook her head and smiled. "I forgot what a poet and a philosopher you are."

She kissed him on the cheek, feeling as if a burden had washed down her back just as the water washed down Weeping Wall. Hand in hand, she and Brian returned to where the others were walking along the Big Bend pullout.

On their last night, they went to the casino on the reservation, where they ran into Karen and Terry Murray.

The couple looked happy together at the blackjack table. When Ellen and her friends invited Karen and Terry to come by and see the renovated house, she noticed that Terry was drinking water.

It was while they were visiting with the Murrays that Sue had a strike of inspiration. Instead of hoarding the vacation home between themselves, Sue and her friends should rent it out to others, so the tourists could learn about the historical building, the land, and its stories, too. It would be an opportunity for visitors to the area to learn about Blackfeet history. Plus, the rental income would pay for the hiring of a property manager.

"And I know just who should manage it," Sue said. "Rich Falcon."

"I trust him completely," Tanya said.

Ellen turned to Karen. "Do you think he'd agree to do it?"

"To have the chance to supplement his tour business while educating others about our traditions?" Karen asked. "I think he'd be thrilled."


Ellen and Brian flew together from Montana to San Antonio, where Brian would stay for another few days before heading back to Portland. They had just walked in with their luggage when Ellen's phone rang.

"It's Nolan," she said to Brian before answering.

"Mom, I have news," Nolan said.

"Tell me," she said. "Are you moving back to Texas?"

"As a matter of fact, we are," he said.

"What? I was only kidding, like I always do. But you're serious? Please say you're serious!"

"I'm serious," Nolan said. "I got a job at North Central Baptist Hospital in San Antonio."

"That's where you were born!" Ellen shouted with glee. "Oh, sweet boy. I can't believe it!"

"We have more news," Taylor said into the phone.

"You found a house?" Ellen guessed.

"Not yet," Taylor said. "We're pregnant."

Ellen froze, trying to grasp what she'd just been told. Her son and his wife were moving back to San Antonio from Oklahoma *and* they were pregnant?

"Mom? You're going to be a grandmother!"

Tears flooded Ellen's eyes, and she couldn't speak.

Brian took the phone, laughing and said, "Your mother is so happy, so very happy, that she can't even talk."

Nolan's wife gave birth to a baby girl in mid-November. Sue and Tanya had gone to wait with Ellen at the hospital and were among the first to see her.

As soon as Ellen saw the tiny little bundle, she was in love.

"Oh, Ellen," Tanya said. "I'm so jealous."

"Me, too," Sue said. "I need to tell Lexi and Stephen to get on the ball."

"You'll both have grandchildren of your own soon enough, I'm sure," Ellen said, trying not to gloat.

Once Sue and Tanya had left, Ellen took a short break from helping Taylor and Nolan with the baby to call Brian with the news.

After he congratulated her, he said, "There's something I've been wanting to talk to you about."

"Oh? What, Brian?"

"I don't like missing these important moments in your life. How would you feel about me moving to San Antonio? I could get my own place, if you're not ready…"

"I'm ready," she said with tears in her eyes. "Move in with me Brian. Move in with me as soon as you can."

"I don't want to risk ruining the moment by asking you one more thing, but…"

"Yes. Let's do it."

"How do you know what I was going to ask? What if I asked you to parachute from an airplane with me?"

Ellen laughed. "Oh, Brian. I'm game for whatever you want. If you're here with me, sharing my life, I'm game for anything."

"Even marriage?" he asked.

"Especially that."

In late December, Ellen and Brian treated the whole family to a trip to Montana, where they stayed at Talks to Buffalo Lodge for a white Christmas. They gave Nolan, Taylor, and little Brianna the master. Alison and Lane shared one of the upstairs rooms, and Ellen and Brian shared the other. Together, they decorated a tree, cooked a meal, and celebrated Christmas with carols and the exchange of gifts. At the end of their celebration, Ellen and Brian announced their engagement to the rest of the family.

Ellen was relieved when her children embraced them and told them how happy they were. Their words of congratulations seemed genuine. Like Ellen, they could appreciate Paul's presence watching over them while still being able to move forward in life.

Later that evening, while Ellen, Alison, and Brian were cleaning up in the kitchen, and Lane, Nolan, and Taylor were playing with Brianna on the living room floor, Ellen felt the most profound sense of calm wash over her. Crow Woman and Rabbit had definitely moved on, and so had Ellen. All three of them had finally taken steps to boldly go where they'd never gone before, and what they found waiting for them was pure, unadulterated joy.

## THE END

Thank you for reading my story. I hope you enjoyed it! If you did, please consider leaving a review. Reviews help other readers to discover my books, which helps me.

Please visit my website at evapohler.com to get the next book, *The Shade of Santa Fe.*

Here's the blurb:

**A haunting in Santa Fe will either reunite Ghost Healers, Inc. or disband the group forever.**

When Ellen decides to buy a fixer-upper in an art community in Santa Fe, New Mexico, she's not terribly surprised to discover that not all of its residents have vacated the premises. At first, she tries to resolve the problem on her own, but what she uncovers about the house's past is so shocking, that she calls on reinforcements by soliciting the help of Tanya and Sue. Can the reunion of Ghost Healers, Inc. untether the troubling spirits in Ellen's fixer-upper, or will their discoveries be too much for them this time?

.

# EVA POHLER

Eva Pohler is a *USA Today* bestselling author of over thirty novels in multiple genres, including mysteries, thrillers, and young adult paranormal romance based on Greek mythology. Her books have been described as "addictive" and "sure to thrill"—*Kirkus Reviews*.

To learn more about Eva and her books, and to sign up to hear about new releases, and sales, please visit her website at www.evapohler.com.

www.ingramcontent.com/pod-product-compliance
Lightning Source LLC
Chambersburg PA
CBHW051938030225
21332CB00043B/1120